**Cumbria**
**County Council**

cumbria.gov.uk/libraries

## Library books and more......

C.L. 18F     24 hour Renewals 0303 333 1234

# His gaze locked with hers.

Suddenly, without warning, the world stood still. Lexi found herself drowning in the chocolate depths of his eyes. And when his gaze settled on her lips, they began to tingle.

What would it be like to kiss him, she wondered? To have those perfectly sculpted lips pressed against hers....

He took a step closer and when his hand touched her hair, desire rose inside her.

*Married.*

The word slammed like a shovel against the side of her head. Reality had finally clawed its way through the haze of desire.

This man could be *married.*

Lexi took a step back.

His hand dropped to his side.

**Dear Reader,**

I admit it. I'm a sucker for an amnesia story. This story came to me when I was in Jackson Hole, riding the tram up to the top of the ski slope. The tram operator was telling me about skiers who venture into the "back country" and how the patrol isn't even required to rescue them. My writer's brain started to think—what if someone did just that? What if he got caught in an avalanche? And my favorite part—what if when they found him he had no identity and *no memory*?

This book is special to me because it has its own song. Sometimes when I'm writing I'll hear a song on the radio and it will fit the story. While I'm writing I will play the song repeatedly. This book's special song was "Come Back to Me" by David Cook.

After you've read the book, listen to the song, especially to the words. Then, if you have the time, email me and let me know if you think the song is a good fit. I can be reached at cindy@cindykirk.com

Warmest regards,

*Cindy*

# In Love with John Doe

# CINDY KIRK

MILLS & BOON

First published in Great Britain 2011
by Mills & Boon, an imprint of Harlequin (UK) Limited.
Large Print edition 2012
Harlequin (UK) Limited,
Eton House, 18-24 Paradise Road,
Richmond, Surrey TW9 1SR

© Cynthia Rutledge 2010

ISBN: 978 0 263 23031 4

Harlequin (UK) policy is to use papers that are natural, renewable and recyclable products and made from wood grown in sustainable forests. The logging and manufacturing process conform to the legal environmental regulations of the country of origin.

Printed and bound in Great Britain
by CPI Antony Rowe, Chippenham, Wiltshire

## CINDY KIRK

has loved to read for as long as she can remember. In first grade she received an award for reading one hundred books. Growing up, summers were her favorite time of year. Nothing beat going to the library, then coming home and curling up in front of the window air conditioner with a good book. Often the novels she read would spur ideas, and she'd make up her own story (always with a happy ending). When she'd go to bed at night, instead of counting sheep, she'd make up more stories in her head. Since selling her first story to Harlequin Books in 1999, Cindy has been forced to juggle her love of reading with her passion for creating stories of her own... but she doesn't mind. Writing for Silhouette Special Edition is a dream come true. She only hopes you have as much fun reading her books as she has writing them!

Cindy invites you to visit her Web site at www.cindykirk.com

To my fabulous critique partners,
Louise Foster and Renee Ryan.

This wouldn't be nearly as much fun without you!

# Chapter One

"Five bucks says he's an undercover prince."

Lexi Brennan stood back and watched the older nurse pull a crumpled bill from her uniform pocket and slap it on the counter.

"He's handsome enough," another RN said. "But I say he's a politician's son. God knows we get our share of them in Teton County."

"Put me down for the undercover prince," charge nurse Rachel Milligan said. "Then we'd better get to work."

The staff scattered, leaving Lexi, one of the hospital's social workers, alone at the nurse's station with Rachel and a nurse's aide. During the five years Lexi had been working at the Jackson Hole hospital, she'd lost a lot of money on these friendly wagers. Last month she'd vowed not to participate in another. Still, she *was* curious. "What are you betting on this time?"

"Our new patient, John Doe," Rachel said. "He's been the topic of conversation since the rescue team brought him in yesterday."

"He is super cute," the aide gushed.

"Mr. Landers's call light is on." Rachel kept her gaze focused on the young girl while handing Lexi *John Doe's* chart. "Would you mind seeing what he needs?"

As the aide hurried off, Lexi flipped through the handful of pages. "Not much here."

Rachel smiled. "When a patient doesn't re-member his name or any of his history, it makes for a pretty sparse medical record."

Lexi recognized Rachel's handwriting on the initial documentation. "Looks like you were working in the E.R. yesterday when they brought him in from Teton Village."

"He was lucky," Rachel said, her blue eyes suddenly serious. "He might have lost his mem-ory, but another few minutes under that snow and he'd have lost his life."

"Why skiers venture into the back country is beyond me." Lexi wasn't sure why she found the man's recklessness so disturbing. He cer-tainly wasn't the first hotshot skier to take ad-vantage of the mountain's "open gate" policy. "Anyone who goes through that gate knows they're taking a big risk."

Rachel's gaze took on a sad, faraway look.

"Young men in that late-twenty, early-thirty range think they're invincible."

Lexi wondered if Rachel was thinking about her husband who'd been killed several years ago trying to protect a clerk during a convenience store robbery.

"Medically, John Doe is stable," Rachel said after a long moment. "Once you find him a place to stay, he's ready to be dismissed."

Raising a finger to her lips, Lexi considered the available options. "There aren't many motels that will take a man with no money."

"He's got money," Rachel said. "He had a couple thousand dollars on him."

A couple *thousand* dollars? Lexi had twenty-seven dollars in her pocket and that had to last until payday. She pulled her brows together. "Did they find drugs on him?"

"Nope." Rachel laughed. "And his tox screen

came back negative. My guess is he's just some rich guy who ran into trouble on the back side of the mountain."

"Well, the money will make it easier to find him a place to live," Lexi said, her mind already flipping through the options. She gathered the chart in her hand and walked the few steps to the patient's room. "I guess it's time to meet Mr. John Doe."

"Prepare to be dazzled."

Lexi paused. "What are you talking about?"

"I forgot to mention the most important part," Rachel said. "Not only does he have money, he's gorgeous. That's why my bet is undercover prince."

*Gorgeous. Undercover prince.*

Lexi pushed open the door. John Doe's money and looks weren't going to help him get a room. That would take luck and a lot of phone calls.

And if the weather reports were accurate, a late spring blizzard was bearing down on Jackson Hole. That meant her focus needed to be on finding this man without a memory a place to stay sooner rather than later.

John had just pulled on his ski pants and had a shirt in hand when a knock sounded at his hospital room door. "Come in."

He didn't bother to look when the door opened, knowing his visitor would be another nurse, wanting to check his pupils and blood pressure. But at the click of heels on the tile, he turned.

The woman striding into his room didn't have on scrubs. Instead she wore a stylish green-and-brown dress with a short green sweater. Her dark hair hung loose to her shoulders in a sleek bob, and her amber-colored eyes were focused on the chart in her hand.

When she finally looked up, her eyes widened. "I'm sorry," she stammered, stepping back. "I didn't realize you were dressing. I'll come back later."

He dropped his gaze to his bare chest then back to the two bright spots of pink dotting her cheeks.

No, he decided, this one was definitely not a nurse.

Her hand reached behind her for the doorknob.

"Don't leave." With one quick movement he pulled the turtleneck over his head, ignoring the fierce ache in his neck and shoulders. That pain, the doctor told him, was to be expected. "There. I'm dressed and ready for visitors."

The woman dropped her hand to her side. She

smiled, showing a mouthful of perfect white teeth. "I'm Lexi Brennan, one of the hospital social workers and part of the discharge planning team."

She crossed the room. When she drew close and extended her hand, he inhaled the light floral scent of her perfume.

The grip was firm, her gaze direct. He found himself glancing at her hand—as if it had been his habit—and noted she wasn't wearing a wedding ring.

"Mr.….Doe. I've been charged with finding you a place to live." Her expression was serious and all business. "Somewhere you can stay until you regain your memory."

He thought of a dozen quips that might make her smile again. The trouble was he didn't feel like joking.

This darkness in his head annoyed him.

Okay, it had him worried. His rescuers had reported that when they'd pulled him out from under the snow, he'd been talking and joking. It wasn't until they'd taken him to the clinic at the bottom of the hill that they'd realized he didn't know who he was...or even if he'd been skiing alone. Only the news that his transceiver had been the only one emitting signals reassured him.

Still, he wished he knew for certain. "Has anyone showed up?"

A look of confusion settled on the social worker's pretty face. "Showed up?"

"You know...family, friends."

Lexi could see the frustration on his face and hear it in his tone. She offered a sympathetic smile. "They probably haven't heard the news yet. Your ordeal was on local television news last night. My understanding is they plan to run the piece again today. And the hospital is putting together a press release that will be sent out if no one comes forth by tomorrow."

He began to pace, finally stopping at a window overlooking the Elk Refuge. "What am I supposed to do in the meantime?"

Lexi didn't have an answer. She placed her leather portfolio on the closest table and moved to his side. The endless sky had turned cloudy as if picking up on the mood inside the hospital room.

"The forecasters are predicting a blizzard." Lexi held to the tenet that when in doubt talk about the weather. "We don't get many this late in April."

Lexi felt his gaze on her and her body prickled with awareness. He smelled clean, like soap and some other indefinable male scent. Rachel had been right. He *was* dazzling. Standing just over six feet with a lean muscular build and dark hair brushing his collar, he was just the size she liked. Coupled with a face that could easily grace the cover of any magazine, he was one potent package.

"When is it supposed to hit?" he asked.

Lexi faced him. "It's supposed to start snowing this afternoon and continue throughout the night."

"The doctors say there's nothing more they can do for me."

His tone gave little away and if Lexi hadn't been looking directly at him, she'd have missed the momentary flash of fear in his brown eyes.

She offered him a reassuring smile. "Look at this move as the next step on the journey back to your old life."

"I'm certainly not remembering my past by sitting and looking at these four walls." He glanced around the hospital room. "I'm ready to get out of here."

Lexi wondered if he was trying to reassure her or himself. She couldn't begin to imagine how scary it would be to think of going out into the world with no memory. Her heart softened. "I'll make some calls to hotels in the area. See what they have available."

"Can I help? I mean, it's not like I have anything else to do." He flashed a smile. "Besides, this is my problem, not yours."

Lexi steeled herself against the mesmerizing warmth of those chocolate-brown eyes. "That's kind of you. But finding you a place to stay is my job. And I'm hoping to get you the special pricing the hospital has for patients and their relatives."

"The E.R. doctor said I had a couple thousand

dollars on me when I was found." He waved a dismissive hand. "Money isn't an issue."

"It won't be if your family or friends come forward." Lexi chose her words carefully, not wanting to dash his hopes. "But if they take a while, or if your memory comes back more slowly than anticipated, you could run out of money. Then—"

"I understand," he said. "I could end up on the street and out of money. That certainly isn't where I want to be." He grinned and pretended to shiver. "Not with snow on the ground."

Lexi returned his smile, admiring the way he kept his spirits up with such a heavy weight on his shoulders. John Doe was definitely one of a kind.

While she was immune to his physical perfection, the humor, the smarts, and the level-headed attitude—those attributes were much harder for her to resist. But resist she would. Because there was no room in her life for a man, even one as handsome and charming as John Doe.

Thirty minutes later, Lexi sat back, frustration coursing through her veins. "How can they *all* be full?"

The words had barely left her lips when Rachel breezed into the room. Her gaze slid from Lexi to John. "What's the verdict? Where's your new home?"

"It's seems," John said, bestowing that hundred-watt smile on the pretty nurse, "that there are no rooms at any of the inns."

Rachel's eyes widened. She turned to Lexi. "Seriously?"

Lexi raked a weary hand through her hair. "It's the storm. Travelers who were going to move on decided to stay. Others who were passing through stopped and got their rooms early."

Rachel's cornflower-blue eyes began to dance. "Surely there has to be *some* place that wants him."

"Hey, I'm right here in the room," John shot back. "Thanks for making me feel like a loser."

The two laughed and Lexi felt a twinge of something that felt an awful lot like jealousy, but couldn't be.

Still, the nurse looked especially pretty today. Lexi wondered if John preferred blondes. Not that his taste in women mattered to her. Besides, for all anyone knew he could be married with a couple of kids.

"I've got an idea." Rachel turned to Lexi. "What about Wildwoods?"

Lexi shook her head. "When I left for work

this morning, all the rooms and cabins were full."

"Mrs. Landers had been staying in the lodge while her husband was here," Rachel said. "The doctor dismissed him early this morning and they headed for home."

"Wildwoods?" John cocked his head.

"It's the B and B where Lexi lives," Rachel said. "Just outside of Wilson. About ten miles from here."

John's brows pulled together. He shifted his gaze to Lexi. "You live at a bed-and-breakfast?"

"That's right," Lexi said easily. "And I cook there on the weekends, too."

When she'd been a little girl standing on a stepstool helping her mother prepare meals, she'd never imagined the skills she'd learned would come in so handy. In exchange for low rent she prepared gourmet meals on weekends and holidays. It cost a lot to live in Jackson Hole and a social worker's salary only went so far.

"Sounds like you're a busy woman." John's gaze lingered. Instead of pity or condescension she saw admiration and something else. The pure masculine appreciation lighting his dark eyes took her by surprise. It had been a long time since a man had looked at her that way.

"So, are you going to call Coraline?" Rachel asked.

"Right now," Lexi said.

Coraline Coufal, the owner and proprietor, answered on the second ring. Lexi explained the situation and then held her breath. She wasn't sure whether to be relieved or distressed when she learned there was one room still available.

"We'll take it." Lexi flipped her phone shut and smiled at John. "Congratulations. Somebody wants you after all."

## Chapter Two

By the time Lexi clocked out at noon, thousands of tiny snowflakes filled the air. John stood with Rachel under the front entrance overhang while Lexi retrieved her car from the nearby employee lot.

John shifted from one foot to the other, feeling useless. Though his past was still blank, something told him Lexi wasn't the only one who liked to keep busy. "I could have gone with her."

"If you did, I'd be in trouble. Hospital policy dictates you get picked up here." A brisk north wind slapped them in the face. Rachel shoved her hands into her coat pockets and shivered. "There's her car now."

An older model Subaru pulled up and stopped. The nurse reached for the door handle, but he'd had enough coddling the past twenty-four hours to last a lifetime.

"I've got it." He opened the back hatch and tossed his duffel bag inside before shifting his attention back to Rachel. He held out his hand. "Thanks for everything."

"Four words of advice." Her mittened hand closed around his. "No more back country."

"Don't worry." John laughed. "I learned my lesson."

He opened the car door and slid into the front seat.

Lexi cast him a curious glance. "What did Rachel say that was so funny?"

"She told me no more open gates." He snapped his seat belt in place. "No worries on that account. It was my first time and it will definitely be my last."

The moment the words left his lips, he paused.

Lexi pulled out onto the street in front of the hospital and cast him a sideways glance. "You remember going through the gate?"

He nodded as the memory unfurled. "I stopped and read the sign."

"Was anyone with you?"

"I don't know." He leaned against the seat and closed his eyes against the sudden pain in his head.

Memories were there—fragmented images that made little sense and gave no insight into his past, hovering just out of reach, taunting him.

"The memory may not be as much as you hoped for," Lexi said, almost as if she'd read his mind and sensed his frustration. "But it's definitely a start. My father used to say that sometimes you have to start with baby steps to reach a goal."

John latched on to the change in topic. At this point trying to pluck anything from the inky darkness of his mind was pointless. "Your father sounds like a wise man."

"A wonderfully wise man." Lexi's lips lifted into a smile that lit up her entire face.

"Tell me about him," John urged.

"Why?"

He glanced out the window. Snow already covered the sidewalks and streets in a thin blanket of white. "Perhaps hearing stories about your father will jog some memories of my own family."

"My mother died of cancer when I was twelve." Lexi kept her eyes on the highway and the blowing snow. "I was an only child and we were very close. I didn't know how I could go on without her."

He could almost feel her pain. Had he ever experienced such a devastating loss? It didn't feel like it, though he couldn't be sure.

"After the funeral, I didn't want to get out of bed," Lexi continued, her eyes hooded. "But my father told me we'd get through this together. We'd take it one day at a time. He made me attend school. He forced himself to work. We went through the motions until we both felt like living again."

"Sounds like a great guy."

She sighed. "He was."

Perhaps it was simply an error, but he noticed she'd used the past tense. *"Was?"*

"He was killed in a car accident five years ago." Lexi's voice was matter-of-fact but her fingers had the steering wheel in a death grip. "Icy roads."

"Did it happen around here?"

"In Ohio." Lexi shook her head. "That's where I'm from originally."

"Jackson Hole is a long ways from Ohio." John kept his tone light. "How'd you end up here?"

"The job brought me here. I'd never been to Wyoming, but once my dad was gone there was nothing keeping me in Ohio." Lexi smiled. "Enough about me. Tell me what you remember about *your* family."

"Absolutely nothing." He leaned back in his

seat and massaged the bridge of his nose with two fingers.

Lexi slanted him a sideways glance. "Headache?"

He shrugged. "Comes and goes."

"It's not much farther," Lexi said. "You look so good it's easy to forget what you've been through."

*She thinks I look good.* For some reason the thought buoyed his flagging spirits.

Lexi turned the car onto a graveled drive and John's gaze was drawn to the large log home at the base of the mountain, tucked away in a forest of trees.

"Is that Wildwoods?"

Lexi smiled. "Home sweet home."

"It's huge," John said.

"It's pretty big." A smile tipped the corners

of Lexi's lips. "Last summer we began doing weddings."

"Weddings?" Unexpectedly and without warning, an image of him in a tux standing in front of an altar filled with flowers surfaced. But it was gone so quickly he couldn't be sure it ever existed.

"Destination weddings are all the rage and you couldn't ask for a more beautiful venue," she said. "In the summer the wildflower garden is perfect for outdoor ceremonies. We also do quite a few inside in the great hall. Most of those couples exchange vows in front of the stone fireplace."

Her expression turned dreamy and the attraction he'd felt at the hospital slammed into him with all the subtlety of a ton of bricks. However, for all he knew this woman he found so attractive could have a boyfriend or be married. And…so could he.

"How does your husband like living at a bed-and-breakfast?" he asked in a casual tone.

"I'm not married."

"Divorced?"

"Never married."

"I'm surprised." He was also relieved, but saw no reason to mention that fact. "A woman as pretty as you…I'd have thought you'd have been snatched up long ago."

"I'm too busy to date." Lexi pulled the car to a stop in a small parking lot adjacent to the side of the house.

John glanced out the window, but the blowing snow made it difficult to see much. "Looks like we got here just in time."

"I'm glad I got off at noon." Two lines of worry appeared between her brows. "If it continues falling at this pace, we're going to have a real blizzard on our hands."

"I guess that means we better get inside." He leaned over the seat and grabbed the bag stuffed with underwear, jeans, shirts, sweaters...and all the necessary toiletries.

He'd tried to give the older woman who'd brought the bag to his room some money for the items. She'd refused to take anything from him, but her warm generosity wouldn't be forgotten. He'd find a way to repay the hospital auxiliary for their kindness.

Lexi secured the top button on her coat and pushed open the door. "Race you to the front door."

John shoved open his own door and ducked his head. The wind blew sideways with such force it made walking difficult and running impossible. Though he didn't want to overstep, when Lexi slipped and almost fell, he took her arm. The heels she wore were more suited to a night on the town than a slick walkway.

She smiled her thanks and he tightened his hold as together they climbed the steps of the massive porch. They'd barely reached the front door when it flew open.

A middle-aged woman with salt-and-pepper hair and a worried expression motioned them inside. "I'm so glad you left when you did. They just announced on the radio that the roads in and out of Jackson have been closed."

"The snow isn't the only problem," Lexi said. "It's the ice under the snow and the visibility that makes driving treacherous."

The woman hung their coats on an elaborately carved coat-tree in the spacious foyer and she and Lexi spent a couple more minutes discussing the weather. John lifted his gaze, taking in the high open ceilings and the large windows.

"How's Addie?" Lexi asked.

"Much better," Coraline said. "Whatever she had must have been one of those twenty-four-hour bugs."

John wondered if Addie was yet another patient from the hospital. Whoever she was, by the look of relief on Lexi's face, it was apparent she'd been worried about her.

"By the way, I'm Coraline Coufal." The older woman held out her hand. "Welcome to Wildwoods."

"I'm Jack," he improvised, taking her hand. "Jack Snow."

Lexi raised a brow but didn't say a word.

"Well, Mr. Snow. It's a pleasure having you with us." Her gaze was curious but she asked no questions. "I'll get your key then show you to your room."

As she hurried off, Lexi leaned close. "Jack Snow?"

"Better than John Doe." He inhaled the intoxicating scent of her perfume. "Snow seemed appropriate given the current weather conditions."

"We're in business." Coraline swept into the foyer holding up a large brass key.

"Nice meeting you, Jack." Lexi held out her hand.

His fingers had barely closed around hers when a dark-haired child in a flannel nightgown bounded down the stairs and flung her arms around Lexi. "Mommy. Mommy."

Lexi released his hand and her lips lifted in a smile. She lifted the child off her feet and spun her around. "I'm so happy to hear my girl is feeling better."

"Your girl?" Jack sputtered.

Lexi planted a kiss on Addie's hair then turned the child in her arms to face him. "Jack Snow, I'd like you to meet my daughter, Miss Addison Brennan."

Lexi hadn't been sure how John, er, Jack, would react to the news she had a daughter, but he merely blinked then extended his hand to the seven-year-old.

"Addison is a beautiful name." He took her small hand in his. "For a very beautiful girl."

Addie giggled. "What's your name?"

"Jack Snow."

The child giggled again. "That's a funny name."

"Yes, it is," Jack said easily before Lexi could reprimand her daughter. "How old are you, Addie?"

"Seven," she said proudly. "I'm in second grade."

"That's cool."

"My teacher is Mrs. Kohtz," Addie said. "She told my mommy I'm a smart girl."

"Too smart," Lexi murmured under her breath.

Jack tilted his head. "I heard you've been sick."

"I had a cold." Addie twirled in place. "But I'm all better now."

"I see that." His gaze dropped to her feet. "I like your bunny slippers."

"Mommy got them for me." Addie quit spinning. She lifted one foot and shook it, making the ears flop.

Lexi listened to the conversation in amazement. Addie hadn't been around many men. But she was blossoming under Jack's undivided attention.

"Lexi?"

Coraline's voice pulled Lexi from her reverie. She glanced up to find not only her friend staring, but Addie and Jack, as well.

"I was asking if once Jack gets unpacked the three of you would like to join me for lunch later in the kitchen?"

Lexi's first impulse was to say no. She'd done her job. She'd found Jack a place to live. Heck, she'd driven him right to the door. Her obligation as a hospital social worker had been fulfilled. No one would fault her if she said no.

"Can we eat with Mr. Snow?" Addie begged. "Pretty please?"

Jack remained silent, but the hopeful look in his eyes tugged at her heartstrings. He'd lost his past. He'd almost lost his life. If she were in his place, she'd hope someone would go beyond the call of duty and show some compassion. "I'd love some lunch."

A look of relief crossed Jack's face and Addie gave a whoop.

"I'll show Jack to his room so he can get settled," Coraline said. "Let's plan to meet in the kitchen in a half hour."

"While you do that I'll take Addie upstairs so she can get dressed," Lexi said.

"But I want to wear my bunny slippers," Addie whined.

"You may wear the slippers," Lexi said to her daughter. "But this isn't our home and you aren't going to run around the lodge in your nightie."

Addie opened her mouth to protest, but Jack spoke first.

"You said you lived in a cabin," Jack said smoothly. "Is it far from the main lodge?"

Addie vigorously nodded her head. "It's a long, long ways."

"Not quite that far." Lexi smiled at her daughter before returning attention to Jack. "But I'm sure not looking forward to braving the wind and snow."

"Why don't you and Addie take my room tonight?" he offered. "I can sleep on a sofa somewhere."

"No need," Coraline said. "Lexi and Addie will stay with me. My suite has an extra bedroom."

"What about the people in the other cabins?" Jack asked. "Will they be safe in this storm?"

Lexi realized he wasn't merely making conversation. She'd noticed the man had an insatiable curiosity about, well, practically everything.

"The cabins have fully stocked kitchens and fireplaces," Coraline said. "The guests who stay in them do so for the privacy and for the outdoor experience."

"The ski patrol thought I might have been living in a cabin in the Teton Village area," Jack murmured almost to himself. His brows furrowed as though the conversation had raised even more questions in his mind. Lexi decided to give him a break.

"C'mon, sweetie." She laid a hand on her daughter's shoulders. "Let's go upstairs and get you dressed so we can eat. I'm starving."

"I'm starving, too." Addie turned and looked expectantly at Jack.

"I'm starving three," he said, focused once more on the conversation.

Addie giggled.

Lexi laughed even as warning flags popped up. Smart, charming and handsome. There was no room at her inn for such a man. No room at all.

## Chapter Three

Unpacking didn't take much time. Not when all Jack's worldly possessions fit inside a duffel bag.

Still, he wasn't complaining. The avalanche that had stolen his memory could easily have taken his life. He might not remember anything before yesterday but he had clothes to wear, a roof over his head and in a few minutes he was going to have lunch with a beautiful woman and her adorable daughter.

Lexi continued to surprise him. When she'd blushed at the sight of his bare chest, he'd concluded she was an innocent. One of those pretty women that, for whatever reason, didn't have much experience with men. Then he'd discovered she had a precocious seven-year-old daughter. A little girl who was the spitting image of her lovely mother.

Jack gazed out the window at the falling snow. He'd enjoyed talking to Addie. The conversation had flowed naturally and he'd felt comfortable around the child. It appeared that he was used to being around children. Did he have a daughter? Or a son? He dropped his gaze to his ringless left finger. Did he have a wife?

Leaning forward, he placed both hands on the windowsill and rested his forehead against the double-plated glass. He closed his eyes and willed himself to remember.

But no memories came forward. It was as if his life had started when the ski patrol had plucked him from the snow.

Reluctantly he straightened. The psychiatrist who'd seen him at the hospital had said that he shouldn't try to force his recovery. He was supposed to keep his mind open and let the memories come to him.

The trouble was his mind was wide open and nothing was knocking at the door.

*Give it time,* he told himself. *There might be a good reason you're not remembering.* Of all the things the doctor had told him, that comment had concerned him the most. At first he'd worried he'd been skiing with someone—a friend, a wife, a child—and they hadn't survived.

But when the head of the ski patrol had

stopped by the hospital to check on him, the guy had insisted there hadn't been any other transceiver signals in the area. That seemed to confirm he'd been skiing alone. But why? Especially in such a dangerous area?

Had something happened in his life the day he'd gone to the slopes? Had he fought with a wife or girlfriend? Walked away from his family? Dissed his friends? Was he a jerk? Is that why no one had been with him? Why no one had come forward?

Jack stared out the window at the falling flakes, adding and discarding possibilities until his head began to ache. He massaged the back of his neck trying to ease the tightness. All he had were questions. Not a single answer.

He wasn't sure how long he stood there. It took the loud growling of his stomach to pull him from his reverie. When it continued to rumble, Jack remembered Coraline's invitation.

His lips tipped upward. Finally, a problem with an easy solution. Grinning, Jack headed to the kitchen.

"That was excellent." Jack sat back from the oval wooden table and heaved a contented sigh. "I can't remember a better meal."

Lexi exchanged a glance with Coraline. She tried but couldn't keep her lips from twitching.

"Go ahead and laugh. I'm well aware this is my first meal outside of the hospital." Jack's brown eyes danced with good humor. "Yet, even without anything to compare against, I know good food when I taste it."

"Thank you, Jack. I'm happy you enjoyed it." Coraline rose to her feet. "Believe it or not, it's time for me to start getting ready for dinner."

"I'll help." Lexi started to rise but Coraline put a hand on her shoulder and pushed her back down.

"Absolutely not." Coraline's smile softened her words. "This is your opportunity to relax and spend time with your little girl."

"But I want to play checkers with Sarah." Addie tugged her mother's sleeve. "You promised if I was better today, we could play. You promised. You—"

"Addison, cut the whine," Lexi said firmly before turning her gaze to a clearly curious Jack. "Sarah is Addie's age. Her father is in Jackson on business and she and her mother came with him on this trip." Lexi settled her gaze on her daughter. "You may play with Sarah until dinnertime. After that you're stuck with me."

Addie popped up from the table like a jack-in-the-box. "Can I go now?"

The child danced from one foot to the other, her voice quivering with excitement.

Lexi's heart overflowed with love for her exuberant child. It was hard to believe she'd once prayed that the positive pregnancy test was a mistake. Now she couldn't imagine her life without Addie in it. "What do you tell Coraline?"

The child stopped hopping. Her smile disappeared. Confusion blanketed her face.

"Thank you." Jack spoke behind his hand in an elaborate stage whisper.

Addie's eyes lit up like a Christmas tree.

"Thank you, Coraline." Addie flung her arms around the woman. "Lunch was fabulicious."

"A compliment doesn't get much better than that," Coraline said with a smile.

Addie turned back to her mother. "Can I go now?"

"*May* I go now," Lexi gently corrected. "And yes, you may."

"Yippee." Addie raced from the kitchen without a backward glance.

"Slow down," Lexi called out.

Before the child had even disappeared from sight, Coraline started clearing the table.

Though Coraline had insisted she didn't want help, Lexi wasn't about to sit around and let her do all the work. She'd barely started to rise when Jack appeared behind her, pulling back her chair.

"Allow me," he said smoothly.

Lexi smiled, impressed by the chivalrous gesture. "You're quite the gentleman."

"I guess I am," he said after a long moment. "I hope so, anyway."

Lexi's heart went out to him. She couldn't imagine what it'd be like to be a stranger in your own body.

Ignoring Coraline's protests, Lexi gathered up the glasses and Jack scooped up the silverware. While they finished clearing the table, Coraline began loading the dishwasher.

Lexi had just started teasing Jack that if he wasn't careful Coraline would be putting him to work full-time, when the older woman cleared her throat.

"I don't mean to kick you out." She glanced down at her watch. "But—"

"You need to start dinner," Lexi said with a grin. She knew better than to offer assistance again. The older woman had already made it clear that Lexi was off-duty tonight. "Jack and I will find something to keep us busy."

Once they were in the hall, Jack stopped her.

"You don't have to babysit me. I'm sure you have your own stuff to do."

Even though less than an hour before she'd been hoping for an out, her heart gave a little ping. "If you've had enough together time, I understand." Lexi met his gaze. "But if you're worried about imposing, don't be. If I had something to do, or somewhere else to be, I'd tell you."

"You're as spunky as your daughter." The admiration took any sting from his words.

"I guess Addie comes by it honestly." Lexi twisted her lips in a wry smile. "But if I start twirling around, stop me, please."

He laughed. "What do you propose we do now that twirling is off the table?"

His gaze locked with hers and suddenly, without warning, the world stood still. The chatter from the housebound guests in the great hall faded and Lexi found herself drowning in the dark depths of his eyes. And when his gaze settled on her lips, they began to tingle.

What would it be like to kiss him, she wondered? To have those perfectly sculpted lips pressed against hers…

He took a step closer and when his hand touched her hair, desire rose inside her.

*Married.*

The word slammed like a snow shovel against the side of her head.

He could be *married.*

Lexi took a step back.

His hand dropped to his side.

"We've got a couple hours," Lexi said when she finally found her voice. "What would you like to do?"

"I'm game for anything that will help me remember."

Though his tone was joking, Lexi knew he was serious. She pondered the possibilities as they continued down the hall into the Great Room. Because of the weather, their options were limited. "I've an idea. You know those getting-to-know-you playing cards that were all the rage a couple years ago?"

He tilted his head. A smile played at the corners of his lips. "Do you really think I'd remember something like that when I can't even remember my name?"

Lexi chuckled. "Good point."

"Tell me about the cards." Jack turned to the roaring fire and held his hands out to the warmth.

"It's a deck of cards with questions that each player answers." Lexi paused, trying to think of the best way to explain the process. "The questions are designed to delve into a person's inner psyche and reveal their beliefs. I've played it with girlfriends several times and it's amazing what you learn about each other. And yourself."

"Sounds interesting," he said. "I can wait here while you get the cards."

"Oh-oh."

"Problem?"

"The cards are in my cabin."

"I guess we can scratch that plan." He took a step closer. "Do you have a Plan B?"

He stood so near that Lexi realized if she turned even the tiniest little bit she'd be in his arms.

*We could spend the time in bed.*

A light flared in his eyes and for a second Lexi feared she'd spoken aloud.

"You've thought of something," he said, his voice deep and low. "I can see it in your eyes."

Her heart skipped a beat and she swallowed

past the sudden lump in her throat. What was it he saw on her face? Desire? Guilt? A combination of the two?

He could be married, she reminded herself, more firmly this time. Even if he hadn't walked down the aisle, he could be engaged. At the very least—handsome as he was—he had to be dating someone.

"Well," he prompted. "What is it?"

Her mind searched for something that didn't involve getting naked. She kept coming up empty until it hit her that she had plans for the evening that preceded Jack Snow and the unexpected blizzard. "Would you like to help me pick out wedding invitations?"

Jack stilled, hoping his shock didn't show on his face. He'd sworn Lexi had told him she wasn't engaged or even dating anyone. Or had he just imagined that conversation? "When's the happy day?"

"Oh, these aren't for me," Lexi said with a dismissive wave. "They're for my friend Mimi."

Jack pulled his brows together. The conversation was getting stranger by the minute. "Don't the bride and groom usually pick out their own invitations?"

"You know your weddings." Lexi waved to two older women enjoying a cup of tea at the dining room table before shifting her attention back to Jack. "But in this case Mimi and Hank have come to an impasse. Since the invitations need to go out in two weeks, they decided that I should choose."

"You're serious."

Her gaze narrowed. "You don't approve."

"It doesn't matter if I approve or not." He

stepped aside to let another couple pass. "It just seems to me that if two people supposedly in love can't compromise on invitations they have no business getting married."

Lexi's jaw jutted out. "Selecting invitations isn't an easy process."

*Let it go,* he told himself. He didn't know these people. Who cared if they let a friend— or even a stranger—choose their invitations? But for some reason it *did* matter.

"You and I just met," he said in what he hoped was a reasonable tone. "But I bet *we* could settle on an invitation we both liked."

Lexi rolled her eyes. "Of course we could. This isn't our wedding. We're not emotionally invested in the outcome."

"Cop-out."

Lexi's brows slammed together. "What did you say?"

Oops. Obviously he'd been a bit too direct.

"We'll pretend it's real. Enter into a good, honest discussion and see what happens," he said in a conciliatory tone. "Unless you're afraid to try."

Jack expected an outright refusal or at least a strong rebuttal. He didn't expect her to turn on her heel and head back down the hall.

"Hey," he called out. "Where are you going?"

"To get Coraline's laptop." She tossed the words over her shoulder. "Then you and I are picking out wedding invitations."

Jack narrowed his gaze. "That one is curvy and way too girly."

Lexi opened her mouth then shut it and counted to ten. If she'd thought he was going to simply go along with her preferences, she'd been mistaken.

When she'd placed the laptop on the coffee table in the Great Room and pulled up one of the largest sites for online wedding invitations, Lexi had made a conscious decision. She wouldn't even think about Mimi and Hank's preferences. Instead she'd do as the bride-to-be had suggested and choose the invitations as if they were for her own wedding.

Unfortunately, now there was a male's opposing opinion thrown into the mix. The style had been their first argument, er, disagreement. She wanted fancy. He wanted casual. After much back-and-forth discussion, she'd reconsidered. This would be an afternoon wedding. In a wildflower garden. A less formal invitation only made sense. Thankfully there were some very cool casual invitations.

Unfortunately, there were also a gazillion of them. They finally settled on one with a celery-colored flower and brown lettering that they'd both liked.

Then it had taken her almost a half hour to get Jack to see that there was no need to purchase RSVP response cards for the reception. He'd been adamant that they were essential…until she'd given him the statistics from a prominent wedding site on how few people responded even when a stamped envelope was included.

She'd hoped the font discussion would go more quickly, but so far that hadn't happened.

"The font you're proposing just doesn't fit the casual style of our invitations," Jack said in a reasonable tone that set her teeth on edge.

Lexi traced the curves and swirls of the beautiful font on the sheet of paper she'd printed out. Years ago, back when she'd been waiting for Drew to pop the question, she'd done a little invitation shopping and had fallen in love with this particular font. But Drew had never asked and now the font—which she'd thought might have a second chance—was in danger of being cast aside. Much like she'd been all those years ago.

Unexpected tears stung the back of her lids, but Lexi blinked them back. She cleared her throat. "It's just that way back when I dreamed of a big wedding, I always pictured my invitations with this font."

Without warning, Jack's hand closed over hers. "Then you must have it."

His generosity brought a lump to her throat. But as much as she wanted to take the offer and run with it, this was a joint effort. "No."

"No?"

"You're right. The font *is* too formal for the invitations and the type of ceremony planned. Besides, it's supposed to be your wedding, too," Lexi said. "We'll find one we both like. One that will be perfect for our fabulous invitations."

Fifteen minutes later the selections had been completed and invitations ordered using Mimi's credit card number. Because they needed to be mailed out in two weeks, Lexi chose the rush delivery option.

After writing down the confirmation number, she flipped the laptop lid shut and smiled at Jack. "Thank you. You definitely brought value to the process."

"I don't know that I added all that much—"

"You were a natural," she said. "It was as if you'd been through the process before."

"Perhaps I have."

Something in his tone alerted her. Lexi took her time unplugging the laptop. "Did ordering the invitations jog something in your memory banks?"

He shrugged and his eyes refused to meet hers.

"You can be honest with me."

"I remember a wedding. I wore a tux." His brows pulled together in a frown. "But there were roses on the altar. *Roses.* That doesn't make any sense."

Lexi wasn't sure what the point was, though she was sure there was one. "Roses are a common wedding flower. The long-stemmed white ones are a favorite of mine."

"I detest them. Their sickening sweet smell alone makes me nauseated."

Lexi forced a light tone. "So either it wasn't your wedding or the bride refused to compromise on the flowers."

He didn't smile back.

"I don't *feel* married," he said slowly, his gaze meeting hers. "Don't you think if I'd walked down the aisle, I'd remember?"

"I don't know," Lexi said honestly. "The psychiatrist would be the one to answer that question."

"If I did have a wife, wouldn't she be looking for me?"

"Unless she's an ex." Lexi's spirits lifted at the thought.

A look of desperation filled his eyes. "I want to remember."

"I know you do." Lexi placed a hand on his arm. "But you got tossed around pretty badly in that avalanche. Cut yourself a little slack. Your memory will come back. Just give it time."

Slowly the panic in his eyes receded. "You're right." He gave a halfhearted chuckle. "I wonder if I was this impatient in my other life."

Lexi grinned. "Probably."

He studied her for a long moment. "You're a nice person, Lexi. I appreciate everything you've done for me."

When she rose, he scrambled to his feet. "If there's anything I can do for you, just say the word."

"Flowers," she said.

"What?"

"The word is flowers."

Jack cocked his head. Then a slow smile stole over his face. "I'd love to buy you flowers. What kind do you like?"

"Not for me," she said. "On Monday I have an appointment with the florist in town to pick out flowers for Mimi and Hank's wedding."

"Let me guess," he said. "You need a male perspective."

"Why, Mr. Snow." Lexi batted her lashes and

spoke in her best Southern drawl imitation. "If I didn't know better, I'd think you were psychic."

"You may be right, Ms. Brennan." Jack tapped an index finger against his temple. "Because I already know there's not going to be any roses."

## *Chapter Four*

After a night of restful sleep, Jack opened his eyes and was greeted by a blue sky and sunlight streaming in through the window. He stretched then plopped back against the pillows, reluctant to leave the warm cocoon. While the room wasn't cheap, it was worth every penny.

The king-size four-poster bed boasted both a down mattress pad and comforter and six super-soft pillows. A large window offered a panoramic view of the snow-capped mountains. Last night he'd left the shades open and the falling flakes had lulled him to sleep.

He'd desperately needed the rest. Yesterday had been a long, tiring day. After he and Lexi had finished picking out wedding invitations, she'd taken him on a tour of the lodge. He'd seen the fitness center, the wine cellar and a kitchen that was clearly state-of-the-art. But when Lexi had invited him to join her and Addie for a movie in Coraline's suite after dinner, he hadn't even been tempted.

His head had started to ache again and it had become increasingly difficult to keep his eyes open. He'd gone back to his room, found the bottle of pills he'd been given on discharge and popped one. Once he showered, he'd crawled under the covers. Watching the snow outside his window was the last thing he remembered.

Though there was no reason he couldn't sleep

for several more hours, Jack flung back the thick comforter and swung his legs to the side of the bed. The cool air turned his skin to goose flesh, rendering him instantly wide-awake. He pushed to his feet and inhaled deeply. This was a new day. A new beginning.

"My name is—" He paused to let the name come out of hiding. But the only one that came to mind was Jack Snow, the name he'd impulsively chosen yesterday.

An expletive burst from his lips. How could a man forget an entire life? A total existence? His own *name?* People had head injuries every day but *they* didn't end up forgetting who they were, for God's sake.

Anger and frustration surged. Jack crossed the room in several long strides. It felt so good he did it again. And again. He paced until his sense of control returned. Until he could accept the fact that there was no use getting upset or whining about something he couldn't change. He was just going to have to suck it up and hope either he remembered his past or someone identified him before his money ran out.

At least, there was one upside. Hanging out with Lexi in such beautiful surroundings was an unexpected boon of his memory loss. Not that he could pursue a relationship. Even if he could say for certain that he wasn't romantically entangled in his past life, Lexi didn't appear to be a woman who engaged in casual flings. Once his memory returned, he'd be headed back to his old life.

And that needed to happen quickly. An unexpected sense of urgency gripped his chest. Beads of sweat dotted his brow. There was something he needed to do, something pressing. He gripped the rising tension with both hands and pulled it back down. Then he took a deep breath and slowly released it. There was always something pressing, he reminded himself. That's why he'd needed this vacation.

Vacation?

Jack paused. Now where the heck had *that* come from?

Several soft melodic dings sounded over the intercom system and interrupted his thoughts. If he'd been sleeping he doubted he'd have heard the tones. It took a moment for him to remember that they signified a meal was being served.

He'd skipped dinner, and from the delicious aromas filling the air, Jack had the feeling this breakfast would be as much of a treat as the lunch he'd enjoyed yesterday. Grabbing a shirt and jeans from the drawer, he quickly dressed. He was almost to the door when the sound of bells filled his head. But these were different than the soft dings. An image of a large stone structure with a huge expanse of lawn appeared in his mind's eye. The bells continued to ring and the sound became a melody.

The stone building came into sharp focus. So clear he could see the veins in the ivy covering the white stone. But try as he might, he couldn't make out the words on the sign out front.

The soft dings sounded again and the melodic bells, along with the stone building, vanished. Jack tried to pull the image back but it was gone. Still, he felt encouraged.

Lexi had been right. Getting out of the hospital had been just what he needed to jump-start his memory.

Jack closed his fingers around the doorknob.

He couldn't wait to see Lexi's expression when he told her the good news.

It had to be the storm, Lexi decided. Saturday mornings were always busy, but this one was crazy.

She dipped another thick slice of brioche into the egg, heavy cream, sugar and ground spices mixture before dropping it onto the large cast-iron griddle. Normally two-thirds of the guests stayed for breakfast on the weekend. But today it appeared everyone had de-cided to fortify themselves with a hearty helping of her brioche French toast—with fresh berry compote—before venturing out into the wintery weather.

Despite being up and busy before dawn, Lexi had found time while whisking the eggs with heavy cream to think about Jack. She wondered how he'd slept, if the headache that had plagued him last night was gone. But most of all she wondered if he'd had as much fun as she had picking out wedding invitations.

"More French toast, please," Coraline called out as she pushed open the door between the dining room and the kitchen. "Everyone brought their appetite this morning."

"I've got a batch ready to go." Lexi put on a mitt and opened the door of the commercial-grade oven. She slid out the baking sheet, removed the foil covering and transferred the warm French toast to the platter in Coraline's hand.

"They look fabulous, Lexi," the older woman said. "And the way everyone is raving, they obviously taste as good as they look. Keep 'em coming, my dear. I'll definitely be back for more."

Even at 9 a.m. on a busy Saturday morning

the look on Coraline's face and the lilt in her voice told Lexi and the world that here was a woman who loved her job.

Lexi understood such passion. She felt the same way about her position at the hospital. Initially getting a master's degree in social work had been something to keep her occupied while Drew finished his MBA. They'd talked about getting married after graduation, but she'd long ago realized that's all it had been…talk.

Still, there'd been a silver lining. *Addie.* Lexi dipped another slice of brioche into the egg mixture and dropped it on the griddle. She'd indeed been blessed.

While she might not have a house of her own or a husband to cuddle up with at night, she had a smart, funny, loving daughter and a career where she made a difference every day.

"I thought I'd find you in here."

Lexi's heart rate spiked when she heard the deep voice, but it plummeted when she looked up and realized it came from the tall man in his late thirties standing in the doorway. "What can I do for you, Todd?"

A divorced father of two with a receding hairline and an ego the size of the Tetons, Todd Cox was a salesman out of Idaho Falls and a repeat guest at the B and B. Lexi wished he'd just once consider staying at a motel in Jackson. It would be more convenient for his business meetings and most of all, she'd welcome the reprieve.

She had little use for a man who didn't understand the word *no*. Todd asked her out every time he was in town. Her answer was always the same, but the persistent salesman was like a dog with a bone. He simply refused to give up.

"Hey, beautiful." Todd stepped into the room with a swagger that reminded her oddly of Drew. "How's my girl?"

Jack had been on his way to the kitchen when he saw the guy open the door and call out to Lexi. He clenched his jaw at the familiarity in the man's tone. The door remained open and Jack stopped just out of sight, curious about Lexi's response.

"I'm not your girl, Todd." Lexi's voice was pleasant but firm. "And I shouldn't need to remind you that guests aren't allowed in the kitchen area."

From where he stood, Jack could see the man lounging against the counter, watching Lexi with an insolent smile. He wondered why Lexi didn't just tell the man to buzz off. Why was she being so nice?

"Coraline won't care." Todd took a step

closer, his body between Lexi and the door. "I'm one of her best customers. Not to mention I send a lot of business her way."

Ahh, now it made sense. Lexi was stuck... and not just in front of the stove. She couldn't risk offending a repeat customer. Unfortunately the guy was obviously too stupid to pick up on her "not-interested" signals.

"Is there something you need?" Lexi asked politely. "As you can see, I'm kinda busy here."

"I heard through the grapevine that there's a fundraising dinner and dance for the local food bank tonight at the Spring Gulch Country Club," he said. "We could go together."

"Todd, I'm—"

"I don't want to hear any excuses about the roads." Todd raised his hand. "The plows will have the snow cleared off in the next couple hours. We can meet at seven in the lobby."

His hand was on her arm now and Jack's blood began to boil. A roaring filled his ears. He didn't remember entering the kitchen but suddenly he was there, at Lexi's side.

He slid an arm around her shoulder and brushed a kiss against her cheek. "Hey, Lex. You should have woken me this morning."

Jack caught the look of startled surprise on her face before he turned to the man behind her. Instead of punching him as he'd have preferred, Jack extended his hand and offered up a friendly smile. "Jack Snow. Lexi's…significant other. And you are?"

He felt a surge of satisfaction at the shock on the arrogant man's face.

"Todd Cox." The man's gaze shifted from Lexi to Jack. A suspicious gleam replaced the surprise. "Why is it I've never met you?"

Beneath his arm, Jack felt Lexi's shoulders

tense. Jack lifted a brow. "Is there some reason we should have met?"

Jack swore he heard a low chuckle come from Lexi's throat.

"I suppose you're right." Todd cast one last look at Lexi before taking a step back. "I'll see you at the fundraiser tonight."

Jack waited for Lexi to reply but she merely shrugged.

"I need to check the road conditions." Todd made a great show of glancing at his watch. "I have a very important meeting in Jackson this morning."

*An important meeting?* Jack cocked his head. *On Saturday?*

Todd started out of the room but stopped in the doorway and turned. His gaze settled on Lexi. "One piece of advice. If you want to keep your job, pay more attention to your cooking and forget about the new boyfriend."

When Lexi remained silent, the salesman smirked. "Your brioche is burning."

At the same instant the words left Todd's lips, the smell of scorched egg hit Jack's nostrils.

Lexi whirled. With a shriek she scooped the scorched bread off the griddle and onto a large plate. By the time she dumped the whole batch into the trash, Todd had vanished. This surprised Jack. He figured the guy to be the type to stand around and gloat.

"Can I help?" he asked.

"It's under control," Lexi said between gritted teeth as she dipped then plopped more brioche on the griddle. "And I can take care of myself."

A shiver of unease slithered up Jack's spine.

"Don't you mean you can take care of the brioche yourself?"

She met his gaze. Her eyes flashed amber fire. "No. I mean I can take care of myself. I have for years. I didn't need you to step in and play the caveman card."

Her voice trembled with emotion and Jack's heart sank. His impulsive gesture of support had obviously been misconstrued. "I saw him crowding you. I may have overreacted."

"You *may* have overreacted?" Lexi's voice began to rise but she quickly brought it under control. "You told Todd you were my boyfriend. You *implied* we were lovers."

Now Jack was thoroughly confused. "I got the feeling you didn't like him. If you do, I'll—"

"I. Don't. Like. Him," Lexi said, her voice a harsh whisper. "But I can handle him. And the last thing I need to happen is for rumors to get started about you and me. You'll eventually leave but I still have to live here. Having people think I sleep around is *not* the reputation I want to have when I'm raising a daughter."

Jack swore under his breath. He'd only meant to help her. To protect her. Instead he'd made everything worse. As he gazed into Lexi's beautiful eyes now filled with hurt and anger, he realized he'd screwed up…big-time. The trouble was he wasn't sure how to make it right.

Lexi fought to make sense of the myriad of emotions slamming into her body. When Jack had put his arm around her and done his Sir Galahad act, her knees had gone weak. But he wasn't her boyfriend or her lover. And he never would be. She lived in the real world. She had a daughter. She had to be able to handle what life threw at her, even if that meant dealing with a sleazy salesman like Todd Cox over and over and over again.

"I'm sorry, Lexi." Jack's voice was low and filled with contrition. "I see now that I put you in a bad position. That truly wasn't my intent. I hope you can forgive me."

As Lexi gazed into his warm brown eyes she could feel her anger begin to fade. She knew she shouldn't let him off the hook so easily, but he *had* chased Todd off. And his intentions had been honorable.

"It'll be okay." She waved the spatula in the air. "It's not like he's going to be talking to anyone about you and me."

"Still, I should have kept my mouth shut." Jack gently removed the spatula from her hand and began methodically flipping each piece of bread. When he looked up, regret was written all over his face. "Seriously, you're the only friend I have. I don't want to ever do anything to hurt you."

Maybe it was the lost look in his eyes. Or the genuine contrition he'd shown. Or how approachable he looked in blue jeans. Whatever the reason, Lexi had to fight the urge to take a step closer and console *him.* Which made absolutely no sense at all.

Instead she took the spatula back and moved the brioche from the griddle onto the cookie sheet with well-practiced ease. Keeping her gaze firmly fixed on the food, she covered the golden-brown slices with foil and put them in the oven.

But when she straightened, Jack was right there, standing beside her with an unnerving glint in his eyes. Her traitorous body immediately reacted to his nearness. The blood in her veins began to flow like an awakened river. Desire pooled deep and low in her belly.

An invisible web of attraction kept her feet firmly planted though she wanted to flee. Okay, maybe *wanted* was too strong a word. The red flags popping up in her head were telling her to run—not walk—out of the kitchen. But the waves of testosterone coming off him kept her tethered where she stood.

"I think this is the part where you tell me I'm a thoughtless jerk but say you forgive me." His gaze remained firmly fixed on her face.

"Oh, the kiss-and-make-up part." Her words sounded slightly breathless even to her own ears.

His eyes turned dark as coal. "Kissing and making up works for me."

*Laugh and say you accept his apology,* the

voice of reason inside her head urged. *Then tell him he needs to leave and let you work.*

It was a good plan, but instead of following it, Lexi took a step forward. She'd lectured Addie many times that if you got too close to a fire you could get burned. But wouldn't a brief brush across the lips just to say "no hard feelings" be on the same level as a warm handshake or a friendly hug between friends?

Lexi took a half step forward and placed her hands on his shoulders. Around his neck would be much too personal.

The heat from his body wrapped around her like a favorite blanket. She let him pull her tight against him, his arms closing around her.

Lexi lifted her face to him. "I'm glad you made it out of that avalanche alive."

He smiled, his eyes dark. "I'm glad you were the social worker assigned to my case."

"Me, too," she choked out, finding it difficult to breathe, much less speak coherently.

"So you forgive me for screwing up things this morning?" He brushed back a strand of hair from her face, his fingers leaving a trail of heat in their wake.

The look of tenderness in his eyes vanquished the last of her irritation. "You meant well."

"I did and I *am* sorry." He leaned forward and brushed an all-too-brief kiss against her lips. "Very sorry."

She paid little attention to the words. His warm sweet lips were too much, yet not enough. God help her, she wanted a real kiss from him.

"All's forgiven and forgotten," she said in a low, husky whisper.

Impulsively she pressed her lips firmly against his. For a second she worried he might push her away but then his tongue swept across her lips. She opened her mouth to him and when he deepened the kiss desire, hot and insistent and for so long forgotten, rose up inside her.

She raked her fingers through his hair pulling him even closer, molding her body against his. The hard, firm length of him pressed against her belly. Still, she didn't break off the kiss.

All she knew, all she wanted to know, was right here in her arms. The feel, the taste, the touch—

"Is there more French toast—?"

Coraline's gasp was like a splash of cold water. Lexi wrenched herself from Jack's arms, realizing with sudden horror where she was, what she'd been doing and most of all, with whom.

"I just put another batch of French toast in

the oven." Lexi somehow managed to force a smile.

Coraline's puzzled gaze shifted from Lexi to Jack before returning to Lexi. "I didn't believe it."

Lexi's heart pounded like a bass drum against her ribs. "Believe what?"

"Todd said you and Jack were lovers. I told him he was full of hot air." The older woman paused, a thoughtful look on her face. "Now I'm not so sure."

## Chapter Five

"I'm not sleeping with Jack," Lexi stammered, taking a big step away from her supposed lover. "I barely know him. And you know I'm the last woman to fall into bed with someone I just met."

"The kiss I gave Lexi was a simple thank-you gesture." Jack stepped forward, putting himself between her and Coraline. "Nothing more."

Coraline didn't argue the point, but the suspicion in her eyes remained.

Lexi wasn't surprised. She couldn't think of one person who'd believe there was anything simple about the kiss she'd shared with Jack. Their mystery man might be a great kisser, but he was a poor liar. She tucked the knowledge away and refocused on Coraline.

"Todd has this fantasy that I'm going to be his girlfriend," Lexi said. "That's not happening."

But Coraline had already shifted her attention to Jack. "You could very easily be married, young man. Yet, here you are kissing a woman you just met."

Jack opened his mouth but didn't have a chance to speak because while Coraline might be through with him, she wasn't finished with Lexi.

"I'm proud of the choices you've made so far in your life," Coraline said to Lexi. "But your contact with this man needs to be kept to a minimum."

Warmth stole up Lexi's neck. What Coraline had said was nothing she hadn't told herself. Still, she was an adult, not a wayward child, and she didn't appreciate the chiding tone.

"You're right," Jack said before Lexi could respond. "Though I don't believe I have a wife in the wings, until I know for sure, I'll be keeping my lips to myself."

Coraline nodded approvingly. Her gaze shifted to Lexi. "I better get the french toast out. I think that will be enough, so if you want to start cleaning up—"

"I'll help." Jack rocked back and forth on his heels. Perhaps he should leave. But to walk out the door now seemed like it would be running away, and he had the sense he'd never been a running away kind of guy.

"She means well," Lexi said once Coraline was out of earshot. "She never had any children. She thinks of me as a...surrogate daughter."

"There are worse things than having a mother hen clucking around." A wave of sadness washed over Jack, though he wasn't sure why. Had his mother died? Were they estranged? Otherwise wouldn't she be looking for him?

"I know you're right." Lexi dumped the egg and cream mixture into a plastic container and popped on a lid. "I just wish Coraline would deep-six the matchmaking."

"She'd like you to date Todd." A twinge of something that felt an awful lot like jealousy stabbed Jack in the side and gave a cruel twist.

"What was your first clue?" Lexi straightened and her lips tipped upward. "Coraline has always liked Mr. Salesman-of-the-Year and for whatever reason she can't see past his slick exterior. Though Todd isn't the first guy she's tried to push on me."

"Are you serious?" Jack lifted a brow. "She's a matchmaker?"

"Oh, the stories I could share." Instead of saying more, Lexi laughed. "It frustrates the heck out of her that I'm not interested in the guys she picks out."

"What's the issue? No chemistry?" Jack couldn't help thinking of the electricity that had been snapping and popping in the room when Coraline had walked in.

"That's part of it. I'd sooner kiss a moose than Todd Cox." Lexi wrinkled her nose. "But it's even more basic than that. I'm not in the market for a man. I have Addie to raise. She's my priority."

"You don't plan to ever marry?" Jack could

hear the surprise in his voice. But heck, he *was* surprised.

"Ever is a long time." Lexi sprayed the stovetop with a special blend of cleansers and wiped the surface with a paper towel. "But probably not until Addie is out of high school."

Jack opened his mouth to argue until he reminded himself that whether Lexi married or remained single was none of his concern. In a matter of days he'd be back in his old life. Assuming his family and friends saw the press release that had been put together to draw attention to his plight.

"The press release should have gone out today." Hope rose inside him. As soon as tonight he could be on his way home.

Lexi paused, baking sheet in hand. "Unless the snow delays it."

The snow. Jack hadn't even considered that

the blizzard might present an obstacle. He fought to hide his disappointment but must not have been successful, because Lexi's eyes softened.

"I know you're eager to get home," she said.

"I'd just like to know who I am." Jack raked a hand through his hair. He hated peering into his mind and finding only a void. "When Coraline talked about me having a wife, I wanted so badly to tell her I didn't. But I couldn't."

"It won't be long." Lexi leaned over and slipped the baking sheet into the dishwasher. "You're young and attractive. Once the paper releases the story, the wire services will eat it up."

What she said made sense. Still, the story would come out of Wyoming. Would that make a difference in its distribution? Would the fact that he was found with a wad of money and no identification spark interest in the story? Would the pictures tip the scale? Jack's adrenaline surged. There was nothing he liked more than analyzing a case....

A *case?*

Whatever had been there only seconds before was gone. He pushed hard but couldn't get close enough to get a handle on the memory.

A gentle hand settled on his arm. "What's wrong?"

"I remembered—"

Her fingers tightened around his sleeve. "What?"

"Something about...a case." Whatever certainty had gripped him moments before was quickly slipping away.

"A suitcase?" Lexi prompted. "A briefcase?"

"No." Jack shook his head, which had begun

to ache. "Not an object. A realization that I like to analyze situations."

"Anything else?" Lexi's eyes snapped with excitement.

He thought for a moment. "Earlier I had a feeling I'd been under pressure and I was here on vacation."

"Oh, my goodness." Lexi leaned back against the counter. "You're starting to remember. That is so exciting."

"It's not so much exciting as puzzling." Jack massaged the back of his neck with one hand. "I also remembered a stone building with a bell tower."

The memories couldn't have been more disjointed or any less clear, but Lexi's smile was like the sun breaking through the clouds. "Don't worry about the memories making sense or not. It won't be long until the thoughts organize together in your mind. Then you'll have it all. I'm happy for you."

Jack found her joy infectious and the light scent of her perfume intoxicating. It took all his strength to keep his hands off. Yet, while he may have promised not to kiss her, he hadn't promised to stay away. "You were right. The more we talk, the more things I experience, the more it jogs my memory."

A dimple Jack hadn't known she had flashed in Lexi's left cheek. "I sense a question."

"Not knowing my circumstances, let me say first this wouldn't in any way be a date," he began with a confidence and smooth manner that was as puzzling as it was refreshing. "But in the interest of helping me regain my memory, would you be interested in attending the fundraiser with me tonight?"

"I'd love to go with you," she said without hesitation. "Under one condition."

There was a gleam in her eyes he couldn't quite decipher. "What's that?"

"That you don't mind if *I* bring a date."

Jack cast an admiring glance inside the large ballroom of the Spring Gulch Country Club. Though the beautiful hardwood floors and the tables topped with linen screamed elegance, the chandeliers made from antlers added a distinctly casual touch.

The tension, which had gripped his shoulders, slid to the floor, where he kicked it aside. Lexi had assured him that the event was casual, but he'd been skeptical. It seemed to him that the dress code for a fundraiser at a country club would be at the minimum suit and tie, most probably a tux. Definitely not blue jeans. He'd worried she'd told him it was casual because she knew those were the only types of clothes he'd been given by the hospital auxiliary.

But looking around the room now, he realized Lexi had been right. Based on what he was seeing, jeans and boots were indeed de rigueur for men. The women were almost evenly divided between jean-wearers and those who'd chosen to step it up a notch with a skirt or dress.

Both Lexi and her "date," Mary Karen Vaughn, had gone the dress route. Mary Karen's blue dress brought out the color of her eyes. Lexi's gold-colored dress was the perfect foil for her dark hair. Though Jack hadn't seen every single woman in attendance, he had no doubt he was escorting the prettiest blonde and most gorgeous brunette this area had to offer.

Jack wasn't sure what he'd thought before his accident, but tonight he preferred a brunette on his arm. Of course, right now, he didn't have either by his side. Lexi and her friend had abandoned him several minutes ago to check out the ladies' room.

While they'd been gone, he'd purchased the admission tickets to the event as a way of saying thank you for allowing him to tag along on their "girls' night out."

On the ride to Mary Karen's house, Lexi had shared that her friend was a divorced mother of three little boys and the sister of the doctor who'd treated him in the E.R. She was also one of Lexi's closest friends.

Jack had felt comfortable around Mary Karen from the beginning. She'd introduced him to her sons, her grandmother and her dog, Henry. An RN by profession, Mary Karen had been interested in every aspect of his case. There'd been no lull in the conversation on the ten-mile trek from Jackson to the Spring Gulch Country Club.

The young nurse had asked question after question but Jack hadn't minded. Every time he repeated the story he found himself hoping something in the telling would jog his memory. So far there'd been no revelations, but the night was still young.

"You're looking better than the last time I saw you."

Jack turned. Before him stood a man close to his own age. Dressed like the other guys in jeans and a casual shirt, he shouldn't have stood out but he did. Mainly because this was someone Jack knew, someone he remembered. As if by habit, Jack stuck out his hand. "Dr. Wahl, it's good to see you again."

The doctor gave his hand a firm shake. "Please, call me David."

"You can call me Jack Snow," he said with a grin. "John Doe was too pedestrian for my tastes."

"I firmly support a man's right to choose his own temporary name." David smiled. "How's the memory coming?"

Jack shrugged, doing his best not to let his impatience show. "Bits and pieces. Nothing substantial."

"You're the one who had the skiing accident." The man standing next to David was tall and thin with a mop of unruly sandy-colored hair.

"When my wife's not here, my manners seem to go out the window." David chuckled. "Jack Snow, this is Travis Fisher. Travis is also a physician, but not the kind you'll ever need."

At Jack's curious look Travis smiled. "My specialty is obstetrics."

As the three talked Jack realized not only was

he at ease in social situations but he could discuss sports without missing a beat.

"So you guys came alone?" he asked, keeping an eye out for Lexi and Mary Karen as more and more people began to stream into the great room.

"My wife is home with our son nursing a sore ankle," David said, an extra warmth to his voice that hadn't been there moments before. "She's a wildlife photographer and those backwoods trails can be treacherous."

"David hated to leave his cozy little family but his wife told him she was sick of all the lovebird stuff and needed some alone time," Travis said, deadpan.

David laughed out loud. "No. That's your ex-girlfriend's line."

"Travis Fisher. Are you stirring up trouble again?" Mary Karen teased.

Jack slid his gaze past the dark-haired beauty to the pretty blonde. "I've got our tickets."

"Those tickets are fifty dollars each," Mary Karen protested. "You didn't have to do that."

Jack smiled. "I'm your escort. A gentleman doesn't allow a lady to pay."

Travis's blonde brows pulled together. His gaze shifted from Mary Karen to Jack then back to Mary Karen. "You came with him?"

Lexi didn't wait for her friend to answer. She looped her arm through Mary Karen's and then took Jack's arm. "The *three* of us are here together."

The tense set to Travis's jaw eased. Although Lexi's friend had made it clear on the way over that, like Lexi, she was too busy to date, it appeared that wasn't from lack of interest. Dr. Fisher clearly had designs on the pretty divorcée.

"Is July feeling better?" Lexi asked David, her eyes filled with concern.

"The swelling in her ankle is almost gone," the doctor said. "She planned to come tonight, but Adam came down with the sniffles. I wanted to stay home, too, but I'm accepting one of the awards on behalf of the hospital tonight."

"Jackson Hole Memorial is a big supporter of community endeavors," Lexi explained. "The hospital and several other large donors are being recognized for their contributions."

*Food bank. Hospital. Donors.*

None of it seemed the least bit familiar to Jack. Whatever he'd done, he'd bet money it hadn't been anything in the health-care or non-profit arena.

"Where are you two sitting?" Mary Karen

asked her brother as they made their way into the crowded ballroom.

"We're not telling." Travis flashed an impudent smile.

"That's okay," Mary Karen said with a nonchalant shrug. "If you don't want two beautiful women sitting with you, it's definitely your loss."

"We're at that table." David gestured with his head toward a large one just off the dance floor.

Mary Karen's gaze lingered on the tented sign in the middle of the table. "It's reserved."

"For award recipients and their families," David said. "You qualify."

The band swung into a song well-suited to the over-sixty crowd. Travis held out a hand to Mary Karen. "Dance with me?"

"Since I don't have any better offers…" Mary

Karen ignored his hand but turned toward the dance floor.

Travis merely grinned and let her lead the way.

"If you two will excuse me," David said. "I need to talk to the food bank director and get an update on the awards ceremony."

This left Jack alone with Lexi. Though they'd come to the event in the same vehicle, he wasn't sure how much togetherness she wanted. Still, it never hurt to ask. "Would you care to dance?"

Lexi nodded and Jack exhaled the breath he hadn't realized he'd been holding. It wasn't until they stepped onto the dance floor that he hesitated. "I have a confession to make."

Lexi stopped and lifted a brow.

"I'm not sure I know how to dance," he admitted.

To his surprise Lexi didn't appear overly concerned. She took one hand in hers and placed his other on her hip. "I guess that means we're going to live dangerously tonight."

Three songs later, Lexi realized *dangerous* was too mild a word for what she was feeling. Up until now she'd kept the conversation general, hoping the impersonal nature of the topics would help. Though it hadn't worked so far, she wasn't giving up.

"You lied to me," she said as he skillfully maneuvered her around the shiny hardwood. Though she'd feared she might have to lead, that hadn't been necessary. "You're a fabulous dancer."

"I guess it's like riding a bike," he said with a smile that sent her pulse racing. "Some things you never forget."

She forced her attention away from his luscious lips. "Has being here tonight brought back any new memories?"

"This dancing, talking, mingling stuff feels familiar and comfortable," he said. "Whatever I did in my previous life must have involved socializing."

She had no doubt that the socializing had involved beautiful women. What she didn't know was if one of those women was a girlfriend… or a wife.

"It has to be frustrating," Lexi said. "Trying to build a picture of what your life used to be with so few clues."

"It bothers me sometimes more than others." Despite his offhand tone, the haunted look was back in his eyes. He slowed his steps until they were barely moving on the edge of the dance floor.

"I wish I could wave a magic wand and your

memory would be back," she said, ignoring the tiny voice that warned once he discovered his identity he'd be gone.

Jack released her hand and lifted his hand to cup her cheek. "You are the sweetest woman I know."

"Face it," Lexi said in a teasing tone, swallowing past the sudden lump in her throat. "I'm one of the few women you know."

His eyes never left hers, though his hand dropped to his side. "Even so…"

"Break it up," Travis ordered, dancing up beside them and stopping.

"Time to switch partners," Mary Karen said brightly when Travis released his hold on her and opened his arms to Lexi.

Jack took Lexi's arm. But he immediately realized it was unnecessary. She'd made no move to step away.

"Not now," he said to Travis. "Perhaps later."

Lexi gasped as Jack whirled her across the dance floor. "What are you doing?"

"They didn't really want to switch," Jack said, feeling good about his decision. "Neither did I."

Lexi focused on his first comment and ignored his last. "They didn't?"

"Nope. The only one Travis wants to spend time with is Mary Karen."

*Just like the only one I want to spend time with is you,* Lexi thought to herself. She'd long suspected that Travis was interested in the single mother. But Mary Karen kept insisting they were just old friends. "Mary Karen was the one who asked to switch."

Jack chuckled. "The two of them are playing games with each other. I chose not to participate."

Somehow Lexi managed to keep the smile

on her face. For a second she'd thought he'd turned Mary Karen down because he wanted to keep her in his arms. Instead it had all been about Mary Karen and Travis. She told herself she should be happy he wasn't beguiled by her charms. Instead all she felt was disappointed.

## Chapter Six

"I learned something tonight," Jack slowed to a stop when the rousing two-step ended. "I love this kind of music."

Lexi had grown up dancing but she hadn't learned to two-step until she'd moved to Jackson. Over the years she'd become proficient. Perhaps even better than proficient.

Jack was a pro. With him as her partner, she'd danced better than she ever had before and had great fun doing it. Though her breath came in short puffs and her heart raced, she couldn't keep a smile off her face.

She waited for the band to start up again but instead, the head of the food bank stepped to the microphone and announced it was time for dinner.

"You're really good," Lexi said to Jack as they headed back to the tables along with the rest of the crowd.

Jack cupped her elbow protectively as they maneuvered through the people. "Another talent to add to my résumé."

Though he was obviously trying to keep it light, something in his tone told Lexi he was still frustrated by an inability to bring his memory back by sheer force of will. She slipped her arm through his. "It's new information. It may not be your name, but it's something."

"I know," he said. "I just wish it would come faster."

"Pastor Schmidt—he's the minister at my church—recently said something in a sermon that resonated with me," Lexi said. "Three months ago I'd asked Addie's father to release all claim to her. So far he's ignored the request."

"Were parental rights ever established?"

Lexi waved the question aside. "The point is I was feeling frustrated like you are now over something that I couldn't control. When I heard the minister say that things happen in God's time, not our own, it spoke to me."

Jack's brows pulled together. "So you're saying I need to turn the timing of all this over to God? Assuming I believe in God, of course."

"Actually." Lexi stopped at the table and waited for Jack to pull out the chair. "I was thinking more in terms of you not driving yourself crazy over something you can't control. Instead of stewing over your memory loss, make a decision to enjoy your time here, however long that ends up being."

"I enjoy my room at Wildwoods." He took a seat in the chair next to her, his gaze firmly fixed on her face. "And I'm enjoying spending time with you."

Lexi felt herself responding to his closeness, to the charm he seemed to have in endless abundance. Then she reminded herself that this was a handsome man. For him, making a woman feel as if she were the most important thing in his world was probably second nature.

"I'm happy you're happy." Lexi inwardly cringed at her sophomoric response. *Sheesh.* She took a deep breath, ignored her rapidly beating heart and tried to remember her point.

"Perhaps you're here to discover something about yourself. Or it could be simply to give your body and mind a chance to relax and re-charge."

To her surprise, Jack appeared to be mulling over her words. But before he could respond, the others arrived. David took a seat, quickly followed by Mary Karen and Travis. They brought with them John and Kayla Simpson, who were friends from the community.

The conversation flowed easily over dinner, the topic of Jack's amnesia forgotten. Lexi experienced a surge of pride during the awards. She couldn't believe all the people in the community who'd stepped up during the past year to help the less fortunate in Jackson Hole.

Unlike some of the attendees in the audience who continued to chat with the person next to them, Jack listened to the speakers, his expression serious. When the food bank employees passed around a ten-gallon hat for additional donations, Lexi watched Jack surreptitiously toss in a hundred-dollar bill.

While she was impressed by his generosity, she thought about telling him he better watch his money. But she bit her tongue before the words could slip out. After all, she was his friend. Not his mother.

After the presentations and another hour of dancing, Mary Karen announced in an off-hand tone that Travis had offered to drop her off at home.

"Will I see you in church tomorrow?" Mary Karen asked while slipping her arms into the sleeves of the coat Travis had retrieved.

"Addie and I'll be there." Lexi slanted a side-ways look at Jack. "You're welcome to join us."

He paused for a moment then nodded. "I'll

take you up on that offer. The more experiences I have, the more chance something will jog my memory."

*And then you'll be gone.*

The realization brought with it a twinge of sadness. She'd enjoyed the time she'd spent with Jack. While she firmly believed a woman didn't need a man in her life to be happy, being a part of a couple tonight had been fun.

After Mary Karen and Travis's aborted attempt to cut in, no one else had tried. Though Lexi wasn't sure of the reason, she liked to think it was because she and Jack looked like they were having so much fun together. They'd even bumped into Todd and his partner on the dance floor. The salesman had simply said hello. After that, Lexi had been able to relax and have a good time.

There'd been no worries that Jack might misread her friendliness and think she wanted more. She'd made it clear that Addie was her priority. He'd made it clear that once he found out who he was he'd be leaving. Even if she was willing to take a chance, the fact that he didn't know who he was or what family he had waiting for him made him off limits. No matter how nice he was or how good he could two-step.

Jackson Hole Christian church was small, old and packed to the rafters. Jack hadn't been sure what to expect when he'd walked through the arched doorway. So far only the band by the pulpit seemed familiar.

"Does this spark any memories?" Lexi asked when he slid in the pew beside her. She waved to Addie, sitting with the children's choir to the left of the pulpit.

"My first thought was how small it is," Jack said. "Then I wondered where they were hiding the high-tech video equipment."

For a second she thought he was joking, until she saw the serious look in his eyes.

Lexi took the hymnal from the rack on the back of the pew in front of them. "Sounds like you've experienced a megachurch. They had those large churches where I come from in Ohio, but I don't believe there's a single one in the entire state of Wyoming."

"Are you implying I'm not from here?" he teased.

Lexi rolled her eyes. "I think that's already been established."

Jack opened his mouth but shut it when the pastor took the pulpit and asked them to rise for the first hymn.

Though the song wasn't familiar, Jack discovered he could carry a tune and read music. And while the service wasn't familiar, he had no difficulty following along.

His favorite part came when the children's choir sang. When Addie rose, her angelic smile seemed directed at him as well as her mother. After one song, the choir director singled Addie out to do a small solo. Jack held his breath. When she sang each note pitch perfect, he wanted to cheer.

The sermon was all about being still so you could hear God speak to you. Jack listened with only half an ear. Today his story and picture would hit the news wires and the Internet. By tomorrow, he'd probably know who he was and be headed back to his home.

"I'm going to add an extra prayer request this morning," the minister said, his expression suddenly grave. "I don't have many details. All

I know is there was an attempted terrorist attack on a water treatment plant this morning in Michigan."

A gasp rose up from those in the pews and the room began to hum with conversation.

A sinking feeling swept over Jack. He shifted his gaze to Lexi. When he saw the sadness on her face, he reached over and took her hand, offering a comforting squeeze.

"There will undoubtedly be more information on this throughout the day and in the weeks ahead," the minister said. "For now let us give thanks to God and rejoice that the scheme was thwarted. Please bow your heads in prayer."

Jack held Lexi's hand through the rest of the service, only releasing it when they stood for the final hymn.

After the service he and Lexi stopped to speak with David and his wife July. Jack was admiring their baby son, Adam, when Mary Karen strolled up. Along with David and July, Mary Karen invited them to join her for lunch at a downtown café. Jack found himself wishing there was time to get better acquainted with Lexi's friends. But Lexi had to make both lunch and dinner today at the B and B so staying longer wasn't an option.

They pried Addie away from her church friends and headed back to Wildwoods. Addie chattered happily the entire way. The child's day continued to go well when they walked into the B and B and ran into Sarah and her parents.

"We're taking Sarah out for lunch and to see a movie," her mother said. "We'd love to have Addie come with us. Our treat, of course."

"Please, Mommy. Can I? Please."

Jack watched her gyrations and smiled. He

wondered if jumping around was a little-girl kind of thing. Kind of like twirling.

Lexi's gaze lifted from her daughter to settle on Sarah's mother. "If you don't mind her joining you—"

"Yippee." Addie grabbed Sarah's hands and the two girls twirled around.

Jack couldn't help but smile again. He was touched when Addie not only hugged her mother but hugged him, as well, before skipping off happily with her friend.

"So what do you have planned for today?" Lexi asked. "Watch the news?"

Jack shrugged. "Not much of anything else to do."

They'd listened to the radio for a little bit on the way home, enough to be reassured that the perpetrators were in custody. But when Addie started to become anxious, they'd shut it off and changed the subject.

The rest of the day loomed before him. It felt weird to be at such loose ends. He had the feeling this wide-open schedule had rarely happened in his other life.

"I have to make lunch today," Lexi said, her smile tentative. "But I'll have a couple hours free this afternoon if you'd like to do something."

Jack felt his spirits rise. "What do you have in mind?"

Lexi held up two fingers. "Snowshoes." She folded one finger down. "Questions."

"Snowshoeing I understand," he said, though it really didn't matter to him what they did. "But *questions?*"

"While we're communing with the great outdoors, I thought we could go over some of those getting-to-know-you questions from the cards I told you about the other day." Lexi shrugged. "Or we can just sit and listen to the news and be depressed."

"I'm up for the snowshoes and the questions." Jack slanted her a sideways glance. "But only if you answer the questions, as well."

"Me?" The word came out on a high-pitched squeak.

"Of course." Though he wanted to get to know himself, he also wanted to get better acquainted with Lexi. But he knew she wouldn't see that as relevant. "Hearing your answers might stimulate some of my memories."

Lexi took a deep breath then let it out slowly. "If you're sure…"

Jack smiled. He was sure, all right. Sure that the day, which had been looking bleak, was going to be a whole lot of fun.

\* \* \*

Jack took to the snowshoes as if he'd been walking on them for years. Lexi had thought she might have to explain how to pick the proper size or at least how to put them on and then maneuver with them. But like he had with dancing, he'd taken to them like a pro.

They stopped at her cabin and he'd waited while she ran inside to get the cards. Lexi had planned on firing questions at him immediately, but instead they'd spent the past fifteen minutes trudging through the snow talking about the B and B and her job at the hospital.

Until it hit her that she'd been doing all the talking. While she enjoyed talking about herself and she couldn't remember the last time anyone had shown such interest in her or her day-to-day life, that wasn't the purpose of this walk. This time was to help Jack get back *his* memory.

"Okay," she said. "Enough about me. I'm asking the questions and you're answering them."

Jack stuck his trekking pole in the ground and stepped over a fallen tree, then waited, eyeing Lexi as if wanting to make sure she didn't need any help.

She stuck her pole into the snow-covered ground for balance and stepped over the log with ease. "Now, where were we?"

Jack smiled. "Question number one."

"These are in no particular order." Lexi had just pulled the cards from her ski-jacket pocket when she caught sight of something out of the corner of her eye. "Very slowly," she said in a barely audible whisper, "look to your right."

A brief look of alarm flashed in his eyes but

her calm demeanor must have reassured him. He slowly turned his head.

The animal sat on an out-cropping piece of rock about twenty feet away, its gaze firmly fixed on them.

Jack's brows pulled together. "What is it?"

"A yellow-bellied marmot." Like his, Lexi's tone was barely audible. "Some people call them rock chucks. They're related to the ground squirrel and prairie dog. I think he's beautiful."

Jack chuckled. "I especially like his bucky teeth."

With an indignant twitch of his tail and a penetrating glare, the marmot scurried back into the woods.

"That's the first one I've seen this year," Lexi said. "They come out from deep hibernation around this time. But I bet the little guy wishes he'd slept longer."

"If he had, I wouldn't have had the opportunity to see him," Jack said.

"That's one of the best things about snowshoeing." Lexi thought about all the wildlife she'd seen on previous treks. "It lets you get up close and personal with nature."

His gaze scanned her face. "You really like it here."

"I do." Lexi smiled, remembering how shocked her friends in Ohio had been when she'd told them she was moving to Wyoming. "I came here for the job. But I fell in love with the way of life. And this dovetails nicely into our first question. 'Are you a beach, country or city person?'"

"City," he said immediately then paused. "I think."

"No, that was good," Lexi said. "You said the first thing that came to your mind."

"How about you?" he asked as they began crossing an open expanse of white.

"Country," she said. "Or rather small town. Definitely."

"But there's less to do in a small town."

"Such as?"

"Theater events. Restaurants. Entertainment."

Lexi hid a smile. He was answering automatically. She needed to keep him talking. "I'll concede the theater and restaurants." She kept her tone light. "But in terms of entertainment, there's a lot to do here."

He grinned. "Like dancing?"

"And snowshoeing. And skiing. And—"

"Point made," he said with a grin. "What other questions do you have for me?"

Lexi pulled out the next card. "Would you ever buy bootleg merchandise?"

"No," he said immediately. "That would be illegal."

"People do it," she said, playing devil's advocate.

"Not me."

Lexi made a mental note of his commitment to the law. "Favorite wine?"

"Domaine Dujac Clos St. Denis 2006," he rattled off. "But the '04's not bad either."

Obviously mistaking her startled look for confusion, he clarified. "It's a Pinot Noir from Burgundy, France."

"It's also expensive."

"It is?"

"About three hundred dollars a bottle." Lexi smiled. "I was looking for a nice bottle of wine to give July and David when they got married. The clerk mentioned that one. It was only about two hundred and fifty over my budget."

"I don't even remember what it tastes like," he said.

"Supposedly really good…if you like burgundy, that is, which I do."

"You should get a bottle."

"Maybe someday. Certainly not in the foreseeable future." Lexi glanced down. "These cards are great. Let's try another one. 'If you could change something about yourself, what would it be and why?'"

"I would trust my own gut," he said emphatically. "Instead of telling myself that something is good when it's not."

Lexi cast him a sideways glance as they maneuvered their way down a hill. "Can you elaborate?"

Confusion mixed with frustration crossed his face. "It made sense when I answered."

"That's okay," Lexi said, feeling his tension.

She'd memorized the next question and moved on to it. "If you could—?"

"Hey, aren't you forgetting something?" He slowed his pace to a stop in front of a grove of trees.

"Such as?"

"You're supposed to be answering these questions, too." He swung his pole in the air and pointed it at her. "If you could change something about *yourself* what would it be and why?"

There were a thousand answers she could have given him. Answers that would make her look good but say very little. But he'd been honest with her. He deserved the same consideration.

"I would be more trusting of men," she admitted. "In my heart I know it's not fair for me to judge the male species because of one bad experience. Still, that's what I find myself doing."

He tapped her pole with his. "I'm sorry he hurt you."

"Well, I got Addie out of the deal," Lexi said. "So I'm the lucky one."

"Still," he said. "You deserved better."

"I did," Lexi said. "But I'm happy with my life. Were you happy?"

"I don't know." He shrugged. "Considering the fact that no one seems to have missed me, I'm guessing there may have been problems. But that's pure speculation. I could have been insanely happy. I honestly don't know."

"I hope you were."

"Someone once said all we really are guaranteed is the here and now," Jack stopped and met her gaze. "Right here, right now, I'm very happy."

\* \* \*

Lexi thought about Jack's response later that evening while she was cleaning up. Addie had returned from her afternoon tired but filled with tales of soda spilled and pizza with lots and lots of cheese. After getting caught up on all her daughter's news, it was time to make dinner.

Afterwards, as was their custom, Addie read to her while Lexi loaded the dishwasher and wiped the counters. Though Addie did a good job with the story, tonight Lexi's attention wandered.

She kept trying to make sense of Jack's responses. He had a strong sense of right and wrong. He was a city guy who liked expensive wine and didn't always trust his own gut.

*The wedding. The roses.*

Had he not trusted his gut and married a

woman who didn't care enough about him to make sure he liked the flowers at their wedding?

A chill traveled up Lexi's spine. She shivered despite the warmth from the kitchen stove. Jack being married was a very real possibility.

"Mommy, am I going to sleep in my own bed tonight?"

Addie's sweet voice broke through her thoughts.

"The walkway to the cabin was cleared this afternoon," Lexi said. "How about we gather up our things from Coraline's then head home?"

To her surprise, Addie hesitated. "Is it okay if I say goodbye to Sarah while you get our bags? She'll worry if she doesn't see me around the lodge."

Lexi hid a smile, knowing it was Addie who was already missing her friend. Her smile faded. She wished she could give her daughter a home with a yard and neighborhood friends to play with. But there was no way she could afford it on a social worker's salary.

"You go find Sarah and say goodbye," Lexi said. "I'll retrieve the bags and meet you by the clock in the lobby at eight."

When Lexi reached Coraline's suite, she knocked, feeling a little awkward after the events yesterday morning.

The door swung open.

"Hi, Lexi." Coraline looked out into the hall. "Where's Addie?"

"Telling Sarah we're moving back to the cabin." Lexi shifted from one foot to the other. "I came to get our bags."

"Come on in," Coraline opened the door wider and motioned her inside. "Do you have time for tea?"

"I wish I could stay." Lexi stepped inside and felt herself begin to relax under Coraline's smile and welcoming manner. "But Addie's got school tomorrow and I've got work. We're heading straight for bed."

"How's Jack doing?"

"As far as I know, fine." Lexi tried not to read too much into Coraline's comments. "We went snowshoeing this afternoon but I haven't seen him since."

Lexi hoped her disappointment didn't show. After all, they hadn't made any plans for the evening. Still, she'd found herself hoping he'd stop by the kitchen.

"You realize it's not going to be long."

Lexi grabbed the two overnight bags she'd packed that morning and straightened. "I'm not sure I know what you mean."

"He'll soon be gone, back to wherever he came from." Concern filled Coraline's eyes.

"Well, while he's here, he needs a friend."

Coraline rested a hand on Lexi's arm. "I worry about you."

"I understand and appreciate your concern," Lexi said. "But I'm a big girl. I can take care of myself."

As she walked out the door, Lexi hoped she could not only take care of herself, but her heart, as well.

## Chapter Seven

The Dallas offices of Delacorte and Delacorte law firm took up the entire tenth floor of Campbell Centre's north tower. During the day the firm—specializing in family law and international child custody cases—buzzed with activity. Between the attorneys, junior associates, countless paralegals and support staff, the phones were constantly ringing.

Attorney Ellen Kloss preferred the quiet of the evening and often stayed late. She supposed she could go home but her nights were way too long already, now that Nick was God-knows-where "finding himself."

A light tap sounded on the glass door of her office. She looked up and smiled, motioning fellow attorney Steve Laughlin inside.

Though dressed in a hand-tailored suit and looking every inch the up-and-coming executive, the tall Texan still had the body of a linebacker. Most of the women in the firm thought he was dreamy. Ellen simply considered the former University of Texas standout to be a good friend.

"What are you doing working so late?" He stopped just inside the door, his tie loosened and his suit jacket slung over his shoulder.

Ellen leaned back in her chair. Steve had been out of town on a case and until now she hadn't realized how much she'd missed their daily conversations.

"I've been reading through some depositions." She gestured to the stack of papers on her desk.

Steve shook his head. A familiar twinkle filled his eyes. "Don't you know that all work and no play makes Ellen a dull girl?"

"I know," she said with a sigh. "But with Nick out of town I don't have anyone to play with."

The minute the words left her lips, Ellen realized how they could be construed. But it was too late to call them back.

Steve chuckled. He raised his hands. "I'm not touching that one."

Ellen laughed out loud. For the first time since Nick had taken off to decide the fate of their relationship, her spirits rose.

"Have you heard from Nick?" Steve asked, his expression nonchalant.

"Not a peep." Ellen did her best to hide her irritation. She hadn't understood why Nick had to leave in the first place. Shouldn't a decision about their future be made *together?*

She frowned. "He didn't tell me where he was going and he's not answering his cell. I spoke with his father in the London office yesterday about a case. He hadn't heard from him either, but wasn't concerned. Apparently Nick told him he might be gone for as long as a month. I don't understand how you can even think about being away from someone you supposedly love for a whole month without calling them."

Ellen stopped to catch a breath and realized with sudden horror that she'd been babbling.

Thankfully, if Steve noticed, he was too kind to mention it.

"I don't understand how he could leave you," Steve said gallantly. "If it were me, I wouldn't let you out of my sight a day, much less a month."

Ellen looked up to find Steve right there. The cologne wafting off him was one of her favorites. She'd gotten Nick a bottle of it for Christmas but as far as she knew he hadn't opened it. "You smell delicious."

His blue eyes darkened for a second. Then he smiled. "Want to grab a burger?"

She'd eaten a fiber bar and apple at her desk. It should have been enough, but suddenly it wasn't. Ellen glanced at her watch. "Do you think Frank's will still be open?"

Frank and Irma's was a small mom-and-pop diner known for their burgers, waffle fries and shakes. Last summer when she and Steve had been working together on a difficult case there had been many late nights. And the diner, just around the corner from the office, had been one of their favorite haunts.

"Say the word and I'll give 'em a call," Steve said.

Ellen opened her mouth, fully prepared to say no. After all, she had a steady boyfriend. But the tiny flicker of hope in Steve's electric blue eyes stopped her. He'd been such a good friend to her. While Nick had forgotten her birthday last month, Steve's gift had been waiting for her on her desk when she'd gotten to work. In many ways Steve had been better to her than Nick.

What would it hurt to have dinner with him? It wouldn't be a date, just two colleagues sharing a meal, like old times.

"Give Frank a call." Ellen reached down and pulled her bag from beneath the desk. "See if that booth by the window is open."

"Walk, Ms. Brennan," the voice called out as Lexi rushed past the two south nurse's station on her way to the stairs.

Lexi stopped and immediately turned on her heel. She smiled. "Mary Karen. I didn't know you were working today."

"One of the regulars called in sick and they asked me to fill in." With three small boys, Mary Karen only worked enough to keep her license current. "July's ankle is doing better so she came over to help Granny watch the boys."

While Mary Karen's maternal grandmother lived with her and helped with child care, three boys under the age of five was a lot to handle, even for an active octogenarian.

"I'm glad July could help out," Lexi said.

Up until a month ago, July had lived with Mary Karen and the two women had shared child-care duties. Since then July had married David, her baby's father, in a lovely indoor ceremony at Wildwoods. Which reminded Lexi…she had another wedding to plan. She glanced at her watch.

"Somewhere you need to be?" Mary Karen asked.

"I have a four-thirty appointment at Petal Creations. I'm picking out flowers for Hank and Mimi's wedding." Lexi saw no reason to mention Jack would be joining her.

Mary Karen's head tilted. "Why are you picking out *their* flowers?"

Though Mary Karen's expression gave nothing away, Lexi could hear the disapproval in her tone.

Lexi had met the twenty-three-year-old Mimi at a hospital "fun run" last year. Her exuberance had drawn Lexi to her. But for some reason neither Mary Karen nor their other friend, Kayla Simpson, had warmed to the girl. They seemed to think Mimi took advantage of Lexi's friendship. But that wasn't the case. Mimi had never asked for anything. Lexi had always offered to help.

"Trying to decide between all the different flowers was causing a lot of stress in Mimi and Hank's relationship," Lexi said in a casual tone. "I offered to help."

"If Mimi thinks she's stressed now, just wait until they have kids." Mary Karen chuckled. "But enough about her. Book club is tomorrow night and you're welcome to bring Jack. As long as he understands the guys will watch the kids while we meet."

"Who's all coming?" Lexi knew John Simpson and David would probably come with their wives, but something in Mary Karen's eyes told her a sandy-haired doctor might also be in attendance.

"You know…David and John and…Travis."

Lexi hid a smile. "Travis is coming?"

"I invited him. Poor pathetic guy doesn't have a social life," Mary Karen said with an exaggerated sigh. "Spends all his time with hormone-ridden pregnant women."

Lexi laughed. She wondered how long it would take before the two admitted they were sweet on each other. "I'll ask Jack. Thanks for the invitation."

"David and Travis liked him," Mary Karen said. "So— Oops, gotta go. Two-fifteen's call light is on. See you tomorrow."

Lexi watched her friend sprint down the

hall. She smiled and turned toward the stairs. Thankfully this time there were no interruptions. Once she reached the main level Lexi covered the distance to the cafeteria in several long strides. Jack had called earlier to make sure they were still getting together to pick out flowers. Hearing his voice on the other end of the phone had been the bright spot in her day. That scared her.

Then she reminded herself that it was only natural. Jack was a novelty, someone new. And just because she enjoyed spending time with him didn't mean she was building dreams around him. She was simply being a friend, doing what she could to help him regain his memory.

The cafeteria came into sight and Lexi quickened her steps. She and Jack were to meet at three-forty-five. She was already a few minutes late. Addie would be at school until five for art club. That meant they had a little over an hour to pick out flowers.

Lexi pushed open the glass cafeteria door, smiling at coworkers but not stopping to chat. Her heart began to pound. She told herself it was because she was on such a tight schedule. But when she saw Jack sitting alone at one of the tables and he looked up and smiled, she realized the way she felt had less to do with time and more with the dark-haired man with the warm welcome in his eyes.

Jack saw Lexi coming toward him. He pushed back his chair and stood. It didn't make sense he should feel so happy to see a woman he'd just met. Last night it had taken all his willpower not to stop by the kitchen to see her.

It hadn't been lack of interest that had kept

him away but rather a desire not to be a pest. Since they'd left the hospital Friday afternoon, they'd been together constantly.

He met her halfway across the room, resisting the urge to reach out and take her hands. "You're looking exceptionally lovely today."

"Thank you, Jack." She smiled. "Ready to pick out some flowers?"

"You bet."

She gestured to the door. "The florist's shop is only a couple blocks from here. I thought I'd leave my car in the lot and we could walk."

He glanced down at the spiky heels that accentuated her slender calves as she walked toward the exit. "Are you sure? Those shoes are pretty but they don't look like they're made for trudging through the snow."

The shoes were eel or alligator, black with pointy toes, a flat bow and spiky heels. Jack had the feeling he hadn't been that observant of woman's fashions, but for some reason he noticed everything about Lexi. Like her shoes. And the way the black-and-tan dress wrapped around her slender curves. And her hair. Instead of letting it hang loose to her shoulders, today she'd twisted it and pulled it back in an elegant knot.

While he liked the look, if they were alone now he'd ever-so-gently untie the knot and let the thick dark strands fall to her shoulders. Then he'd pull her to him—

"Jack."

He looked up.

"The shoes will be fine." The look in her eyes said he was foolish to worry, but he couldn't help himself. She touched his arm. "C'mon, we only have an hour."

Quickly slipping on his coat, he reached over

and picked up hers. "I know we're meeting with the florist. Tell me the plan."

Lexi smiled. It had quickly become apparent that Jack was a man who liked being kept in the loop.

"We're meeting with Delia Juracek." Lexi slipped her arms into her coat sleeves as he held it, then buttoned up.

Jack pushed open the exterior door and an icy blast greeted Lexi with a cold slap across her face. "She's the owner of Petal Creations, a local florist shop. Mimi and Hank met with her last week, so she already knows their budget, the size of the wedding party…that kind of stuff."

Jack took her arm when they stepped into the cold air. She must have looked surprised because he smiled. "The sidewalks could be slick."

"Thank you." Though there was no skin-to-skin contact, merely having him close sent waves of heat coursing through her body.

"So what happened?" Jack asked. "When they met with her?"

Lexi forced her attention away from his closeness and carefully considered how to explain the situation. The soon-to-be bride and groom were nice people. But she feared she'd already given Jack a skewed impression of their character with her wedding planning stories.

Still, she couldn't lie. "Apparently Mimi wanted to special order some flowers not in season. Hank, well, he hit the roof. A park ranger's salary only goes so far. But Mimi has never been married before. She wants everything perfect. I can see both sides."

They'd reached Petal Creations. Despite the cold Jack paused at the door. "Perhaps my brain isn't working right," he said. "But if Mimi wants everything so perfect, why is she allowing a friend to pick out her wedding flowers?"

"She trusts me. She knows I'll do everything I can to make this wedding perfect," Lexi said. "Hank's okay with it because he knows I'll keep it within their budget."

"It still doesn't make sense, but I guess it doesn't have to." Jack reached around her to open the door. "Tell me again what role I'm to play?"

"Just a guy," Lexi said with a wink, "who can't wait to help pick out flowers for his upcoming wedding."

If her job as a hospital social worker fell through, Jack decided Lexi could have a great future as a wedding planner.

She'd come to the meeting with the florist

fully prepared with a list of questions. Oddly, Delia appeared more interested in talking to him rather than to Lexi. Jack wasn't sure why, other than if Hank had "hit the roof" the florist was probably going overboard to make sure he was happy and felt a part of the discussion.

Lexi had even brought along a color swatch of her bridesmaid's dress, a pink chiffon that made him grimace. Thankfully for Mimi, Lexi could make a sack look good.

"The ceremony will be held outside," Lexi reminded Delia. "Since it will be a casual event, I was thinking of a hand-tied bouquet made up of an assortment of spring flowers. For the ceremony itself, a floral arch."

Delia cast a sideways glance at Jack before responding to Lexi. "Would you like to make this color the focal point of the arrangements?"

Lexi's gaze dropped to the swatch Delia held

between her fingers. Though Lexi's expression never wavered, something told Jack that Pepto-Bismol pink wasn't her favorite color. "Lex?"

"I say no," Lexi said. "The pink stands out enough on its own."

Jack nodded. Very tactfully put.

"Have we answered all of *your* concerns, Mr. Snow?" Delia asked.

"The only other concern I had was the smell," he said. "And since it will be an outdoor wedding, the smell of whatever flowers we choose shouldn't be a problem."

Delia sat up straight in her chair. *"Smell?"*

"Jack has a sensitive nose," Lexi said, offering him an understanding smile. "For some people floral scents can be a real issue."

"Good to know." Delia made a note on the paper in front of her. "I'll avoid tuberose, freesia and gardenias."

"And roses," Jack added. "We don't want roses in any of the arrangements."

"Absolutely not," Lexi added, shooting him a wink.

The conversation moved to accessories like boutonnieres and corsages as well as the centerpieces. They scratched the latter off their list. Since the B and B did so many weddings, Coraline would be supplying the centerpieces.

In short order, everything was decided. Lexi seemed perfectly satisfied with the arrangements but Jack still had a few questions. "Can you tell us what kind of guarantees there are regarding freshness, availability and substitutions?"

It must have been a common question because not only didn't Delia act surprised, she rattled off the answers as if she'd recited them a thousand times before.

"Is that acceptable?" Delia asked.

Jack exchanged a look with Lexi, then nodded.

"Okay, well, here's the contract." Delia shoved a piece of paper in front of Lexi and handed her the pen.

"Do you mind if I look at it?" Jack asked Lexi.

She smiled and placed the contract between them. "Two sets of eyes are always better than one."

Delia moved behind him and leaned forward, her breast pressing against the side of his arm. He supposed he should be flattered by her attention, but all he felt was irritation.

Granted she was aware that these weren't his wedding flowers, but she had no knowledge of the nature of his relationship with Lexi. Being flirtatious in Lexi's presence bordered on disrespectful.

"This is our standard contract," Delia said.

Jack scanned it again. "I don't see a repercussions clause."

"What's that?" Lexi asked.

"It would state the florist's liability in the event of a delivery snag." Jack narrowed his gaze. "The refund policy should also be stipulated."

Delia batted her long lashes at him. "I'd be happy to include that…just for you."

Jack met her gaze and held it. The florist must have finally seen what he was trying to convey, because she took a step back and broke eye contact.

"Make sure you specifically state what the refund will be if Mimi cancels the order as well as what Petal Creations will pay if they cancel," Jack added.

Delia straightened. "I always follow through on my orders."

Jack smiled. "Still, we need it included."

"I should have the contract ready for you by tomorrow afternoon." This time Delia focused her entire attention on Lexi. "If you want to bring your checkbook tomorrow, you can sign the contract and we can get the wedding on the books."

"We can stop by and pick up the contract," Jack said. "But the bride-to-be will be the one signing."

"I don't mind—"

"This is a legal agreement." Jack took a moment to consider his words. He wasn't about to tell Lexi what she could or couldn't do, but it was important she understand the ramifications of signing such a document. "If for some reason Mimi doesn't pay—or something else goes wrong—you could be financially liable."

To his surprise Lexi lifted her chin in a stubborn tilt. "I really don't think—"

Impulsively Jack reached over and brought her hand to his lips, kissing it. "Trust me on this one, sweetheart."

"If it were me," Delia said with a pointed gaze. "I'd give the man whatever he wants."

Lexi's cheeks turned a becoming shade of pink. She grabbed her bag and stood, meeting Jack's gaze. "Okay."

"Thank you." His gaze dropped to her lips and the now-familiar electricity filled the air. Everything faded and it was only her and him.

"I had fun." Lexi's gaze never left his.

"Me, too." He took a step closer and held out his hand.

She placed hers in his. For a long moment neither of them spoke.

"Are you sure you're not the ones getting married?"

The attraction that had been building between them shattered.

Jack dropped his hand to his side.

Lexi turned to Delia. "I'm sorry. What did you say?"

"I know these flowers aren't for you," Delia said. "But if you ask me, you guys are a heck of a lot more compatible than the two who were in here last week."

## Chapter Eight

Lexi tried not to think about Delia's comment while having lunch with Mimi the next day in the hospital cafeteria. The soon-to-be bride had been eager to hear about the flowers she'd be carrying at her wedding.

"No roses at all?" A look of disappointment crossed Mimi's face.

With her hair pulled back in a ponytail and not a hint of makeup on her face, the twenty-three-year old strawberry blonde could pass for a high school student. Though she liked to spend money on clothes—she'd confided to Lexi that the ragged jeans she had on had cost over a hundred dollars—she always looked like she'd just tumbled out of bed.

"Lexi."

Lexi blinked.

"Why no roses?"

"Jack doesn't like them," Lexi said without thinking. "The smell drives him crazy."

"Jack?"

"I told you about Jack," Lexi said. "The guy who got caught up in the avalanche last week."

Mimi's brows pulled together in a frown. "What does he have to do with my flowers?"

"I took him along with me to meet with Delia. To give me a male perspective." Lexi sensed Mimi's irritation and found her own rising in response. Darn it, Mimi had given her carte blanche as long as she stayed under the dollar limit. If Mimi expected an apology, she wasn't going to get it. "In our heads, we were you and Hank, looking at flowers for our wedding."

"If it were me and Hank, I would have told him he could hold his nose and put up with the roses for one day."

"Yeah, right." Lexi's smile faded at the look in Mimi's eyes. "You're serious."

"You bet I am." Mimi took a bite of her green Jell-O, scrunched up her nose then moved it to the side of her tray. "This is my wedding and if I couldn't have those imported flowers, I wanted roses."

Somehow Lexi managed to keep her temper in check. "You never mentioned that to me. You simply told me to pick out the flowers I'd like," she said in what she hoped was a reasonable tone. "The only parameter I was given was to stay within the budget—"

"That whole budget thing is really ticking me off," Mimi said. "A girl only gets married once in her life. My parents can't help out. I understand that. But Hank has money saved. Yet he insists we keep this wedding under ten thousand dollars. Get real. This is the twenty-first century. There's no way you can have a decent wedding for that amount. I told him that last night."

Mimi shoved her fork into her mountain of macaroni and cheese with a vengeance.

Lexi wanted to reassure Mimi that she could—and would—have a perfectly lovely wedding for that amount, but the look in her friend's eyes told her there was more going on here than money. She reached over and covered Mimi's hand with her own. "Did you and Hank have another argument?"

A tear slipped down Mimi's cheek but she hurriedly brushed it back. "He makes me so mad. Just because he's eight years older than me and went to college he thinks he knows so much. But I'm not going to just do whatever he wants."

"You're absolutely right," Lexi said in a soothing tone. "Marriage is a partnership, not a dictatorship."

"That's what I told him." Mimi straightened in her chair and punched the air with her finger.

"What did he say?" Lexi tried to stifle her unease. For a couple supposedly in love and on the verge of marriage, the two sure seemed to fight a lot.

"He kissed me." Mimi's lips curved upward.

"And there wasn't much talkin' after that, if you know what I mean."

Unfortunately Lexi did know. In the time she'd known Mimi and Hank, sex had always been the response to any disagreements.

"What's this? This says something about if I cancel the wedding?" Mimi's eyes narrowed on the Petal Creations contract in front of her.

"It's a clause Jack had Delia insert." Lexi kept her tone light. "Just in case something happens and the wedding can't go off as scheduled."

Lexi watched in horror as Mimi struck through the clause with her pen before signing.

"What are you doing?" Lexi asked, her voice louder than she'd have liked. "That clause benefits you and Hank."

Mimi shook her head, her expression turning mulish. "Talking about the wedding not happening—much less putting it in print—is bad karma. I want no part of it."

"But what if—"

"Nothing is going to stop this wedding. I'm not going to let it." Mimi smiled at Lexi, a pitying look in her eyes. "If you'd ever been a bride yourself, you'd understand."

Lexi was still steaming about the gibe later that afternoon when a knock sounded on the door to her cabin.

"It's Jack," Addie called out. "Can I open the door?"

"Yes, you may," Lexi called out, reaching over the back of the sofa to retrieve a shoe.

"Now that's an interesting view," Jack said. "What do you think, Addie? You like the view?"

Addie giggled and Lexi slowly straightened. "Har, har. Hello, Jack. How was your day?"

"Uneventful," he said. "I worked out this morning and remembered a routine I did with the free weights. So I guess I wasn't a total sloth in my previous life."

Her gaze met his. "I never thought that for a minute."

"Yeah, well." He dropped into a nearby chair. "I'm starting to wonder if I'll ever know who I am."

Addie waved her hand wildly in the air. "I know who you are."

"Yes, Addie?" Lexi said.

"Your name is Jack Snow," Addie said, her chest puffed with importance. "And you're our friend."

"Thank you, Addie," Jack said, his eyes warm, "for clearing that up."

Lexi brought a finger to her lips. "I think we have everything we need."

"Not your pie," Addie said. "And I told Connor I'd bring my new DVD."

"Okay, you get your movie," Lexi said. "I'll get the pie and then we should be ready to go."

"What kind are you bringing?" Jack asked.

"Sour cream raisin." Lexi stepped into the tiny kitchen just off the equally small living room and opened the refrigerator door. When she pulled out the pie and straightened she found Jack staring out the window. "Is something wrong? You don't seem like yourself."

"And who is that?" Jack rested his back against the sill. "At the rate things are going, I may never learn my real name."

"You're remembering more every day. It won't—"

"Have you noticed that the only news being

reported is that terrorist plot?" Jack pushed away from the window. "It's the only story on the Internet."

The puzzle pieces fell into place. Lexi finally understood the root of his distress. "You're afraid your story got buried."

Jack met her gaze. "I'm not afraid it got buried, I *know* it got buried."

"It's still out there, Jack," Lexi said. "And I bet in a week or so—if there's no response— the sheriff will send the story out again."

"In a week or so, I'll be out of money," Jack said, a bleak look in his eyes. "Then I'll be out on the street."

"Don't worry about that. Coraline isn't the type to throw you to the bears," Lexi said with a wink. "She'll probably put you to work, but at least you'll have a roof over your head."

"If you don't have anywhere else to stay, you

could stay with us," Addie said, emerging from her bedroom. "Right, Mommy?"

Lexi's smile froze on her face. "Our cabin isn't that big, sweetheart."

"I could give Jack my Strawberry Shortcake bed and I could sleep with you." Addie nodded as if she had it all planned out. "That would work."

"It's a possibility," Lexi murmured, though it wasn't going to happen.

Because she knew if they were in the same house, it wouldn't be Strawberry Shortcake he'd be sleeping with, but her.

Jack hit sensory overload the minute he walked through Mary Karen's front door. Her cockapoo, Henry, was on a barking spree, which had four-year-old twins Connor and Caleb cranked up. Two-year-old Logan was streaking through the house in his birthday suit after breaking loose from Granny Fern after his bath.

John and Kayla Simpson's infant daughter stared wide-eyed in her father's arms, oblivious to the chaos. But David and July's newborn son, Adam, was adding his high-pitched wails to the melee.

"Welcome to my world." Mary Karen reached out and grabbed Logan. "There's beer and soft drinks in the fridge, so help yourself."

"I'll take the twins into the living room," Addie volunteered. "Come on, boys. Wait till you see this movie. It's really scary."

Lexi smiled. "Thanks, honey."

"I appreciate the invitation." Jack glanced around the interior of the older home. While it wasn't elegant, it had a warmth that he found appealing. "You have a lovely home."

"Down." Logan squirmed in his mother's arms. "I want down."

"First you have to get on some clothes, buddy." Travis ambled into the room, flashed a smile at Jack and Lexi then held out his arms to Logan. The toddler flung himself at Travis.

"Fly like airplane," the boy ordered.

"You do the hostess thing," Travis said to Mary Karen. "I'll take care of this one."

"Airplane." Logan pushed up and down in Travis's arms. "Fly like airplane."

"Sure you can handle him?" Mary Karen said.

"Piece o' cake." Travis grinned. "A two-year-old is nothing compared to a woman in labor."

"It's time to fly to the clothing hanger, my boy." Travis lifted the toddler in the air made a sound like an airplane and the two headed down the hall.

Jack watched in amazement. Lexi, or Coraline, or someone had mentioned he might be married with kids. But, based on what he was seeing—and feeling—here tonight, he could rule that out. This was uncharted territory.

"Things will settle down," Lexi said in a soothing tone, as if she feared he would bolt. "C'mon, I'll get you a beer."

Jack followed her into the kitchen. "Is it always so crazy?"

Lexi laughed. "Usually worse."

"This—" he waved a hand helplessly in the air "—isn't familiar at all."

Lexi grabbed a beer for him and a soda for herself. "What part exactly isn't familiar?"

He popped open the tab and took a long swallow. "Any of this," he said, gesturing with the can of beer in his hand. "The home. The kids running around. None of this."

"Hmm." Lexi lifted one shoulder in a slight shrug. "Certainly doesn't sound like you were a family man."

"No, it doesn't." His gaze met and held hers.

"David is here with the pizzas," Mary Karen called out from the living room.

"Why is she yelling?" Jack leaned back against the counter and took another sip of beer.

"Because—" Lexi opened the door to a pantry and rummaged inside, finally emerging with a handful of paper plates and napkins "—she wants me to have these ready."

He sat his beer on the counter and took the paper products from her hands. "What about forks?"

Mary Karen stepped into the kitchen followed by her brother. "We're barbarians," she said with a grin. "We eat pizza the way it was meant to be eaten…with our hands."

The next ten minutes were what Jack would label "controlled chaos." Pizzas were unboxed. Paper cups filled with ice were placed on the counters. Large liters of assorted soda were opened, and everyone dug in.

Somehow Jack and Lexi ended up at the kitchen table with Mary Karen and Travis and the three boys. Addie had chosen to "help" July feed baby Adam in the dining room where the rest of the guests were congregated.

The pizza—obtained from a downtown business—was surprisingly good. Jack was on his second piece when one of the twins sucked milk into his straw and shot it across the table at his brother. Unfortunately Travis had chosen that exact moment to lean over to get more hot peppers for his pizza. The doctor barely reacted when the splat of milk hit him on the cheek.

"Connor," Travis said as the milk dribbled down his cheek. "Four minutes in time-out. Now."

"I didn't mean to hit you." Connor reluctantly slid off his chair to his feet. "I was aiming for Caleb."

"In the time-out chair, Connor." Travis wiped the milk off his cheek with a napkin. "You know where it is. I'll tell you when your time is up."

To his credit, the doctor kept his tone firm, but even.

"Connor's going to time-out," Caleb said in a sing-song tone. "I'm going to eat his pizza."

Like a cobra striking, Travis pinned Caleb with his gaze. "One more word out of you, and you'll join your brother."

Caleb's eyes widened. His mouth snapped shut.

Jack glanced at Mary Karen, calmly cutting up a slice of pizza into bite-size pieces for two-year-old Logan. If she minded Travis disciplining her sons, it didn't show.

"You're good with kids," Jack said to Travis. "Do you have any of your own?"

"Thank God, no." Travis chuckled and took a sip of beer.

"Travis is the oldest of eight," Mary Karen said, placing the pizza bites in front of Logan. "He doesn't want children."

An odd tension filled the air.

"I never said that," Travis said. "Not exactly."

"That's cool," Mary Karen said. "You just have to find a woman who doesn't have any kids and who doesn't want any. Lots of men don't like kids. Right, Jack?"

"I'm the wrong one to ask," Jack said, feeling Lexi's gaze settle on him. "I barely know what *I* like. I can't speak for other men."

"You know I like kids, Mary Karen," Travis said, his shoulders stiff and his back ramrod straight. "Just because I don't want a bunch of my own doesn't mean I don't like them."

Travis glanced down at his watch. "Time to spring the wild man from time-out."

He rose to his feet and started out of the kitchen but stopped next to Mary Karen. "I like your boys a lot. Don't think otherwise."

Mary Karen simply shrugged.

Jack had the feeling it was the best she could muster. He also had the feeling it was time to change the subject.

"My money's going to run out within the next week or so," he said. "So if you hear of any odd jobs where someone will pay cash, let me know."

"There might be something open at the hospital," Mary Karen said.

"Or at one of the businesses in the area," Lexi added.

"I don't have a social security card, remember," Jack said, having already considered—and rejected—those options. "Or any other identification, for that matter."

"I didn't even think of that," Mary Karen said.

Lexi sighed. "Employers need identification."

"Well, if you get desperate," Mary Karen said. "I've got an extra room. You could move in and help me take care of the boys."

"Who's moving in where?" Travis asked, returning to the kitchen with a subdued Connor.

"Jack *might* move in," Mary Karen waved a

dismissive hand. "Nothing definite. It just depends on how long it takes him to discover his identity."

Travis's gaze met his. There was a clear warning in the young doctor's eyes. "If there's any way I can help in getting information out, let me know."

"I appreciate the offer." Jack had no desire to come between Mary Karen and Travis and he had a feeling moving in would do just that. "But I'm still hoping the press release will bear some fruit."

"If it doesn't?" Lexi asked.

Jack's gaze settled on Mary Karen. "Then you just might have yourself a live-in manny."

*Live-in manny, indeed.*

Lexi thought about the comment throughout dinner and even during the book club discussion. Though she knew Mary Karen had no designs on Jack, the thought of the two of them living under the same roof set her teeth on edge. By the smoke that had come rolling out of Travis's ears when Jack made the comment, he felt the same.

She turned off the highway in the direction of Wilson. It was a moonless night and inky darkness enveloped the vehicle.

Addie slept in the backseat, her head lolling to one side. They'd stayed later than Lexi had planned. After their book discussion ended, the kids were in the middle of a movie they wanted to finish and the two babies were finally sleeping peacefully.

Mary Karen had brought out a couple of decks of cards and suggested they play five-point pitch. With four couples they had enough for two tables. Though Jack had obviously never played before, he quickly caught on. Before they knew it, it was midnight.

"I had fun tonight," Jack said, his soft words breaking the stillness. "Thank you for invit- ing me."

"I'm glad you enjoyed the evening." For some reason Lexi thought of Addie's father. He wouldn't have been caught dead playing cards or eating pizza with his hands. "It wasn't anything special."

"It was nice," Jack said. "The kids and the cards weren't familiar, but I liked being part of a couple."

Lexi's heart gave a little ping. "Sounds like that part was at least familiar."

"I don't know." Jack shook his head and she felt his gaze on her. "It was being with *you* that I liked. *That* felt comfortable to me."

"I liked it, too," Lexi grudgingly admitted.

He reached over and took her hand. Her heart flip-flopped.

She pulled back her hand. "I didn't want to."

"Why not?" His tone was cool, well controlled.

"Ah, Jack, you know why." Lexi kept her gaze firmly fixed on the road. "You're going to be gone soon. I can't get attached to someone who's going to walk out of my life and never look back."

"It doesn't have to be that way," he said, the words rushed and filled with urgency. "Maybe we could—"

"There can be no plans, Jack." Lexi tightened her fingers around the steering wheel until her knuckles turned white. "Not until you know if you have a wife or a girlfriend."

He heaved a harsh breath. "But I like you, Lexi."

"My father used to say you have to play the cards you're dealt." Lexi took a deep, steadying breath. "If I had a boyfriend or a husband who'd been injured and didn't remember his name or our life together, I'd hope that someone would be nice to him while he regained his memory. Nice…as in be his friend."

"But no kisses or hugs or—"

"No. None of that." She cut him off before his words could build any more sensual images in her mind.

"Where do we go from here?" he asked in a quiet tone.

"We continue as we have been," Lexi said. "I'll be your friend. We'll hang out and do things together for the sole purpose of bringing back those memories. You'll keep your hands off me and I'll keep my hands off you."

"We'll play the cards we've been dealt," he said, sounding resigned.

"Exactly," Lexi said. "Now, about you moving in with Mary Karen…"

## Chapter Nine

"Did you really think I was serious?" Jack asked Lexi as she pulled onto the drive leading to Wildwoods.

"Weren't you?" The tight clench to her jaw was at odds with her casual tone.

"For a minute or two," Jack grudgingly admitted. He wasn't proud that for those few moments he'd been tempted to disregard Travis's feelings and do what was best for *him*. "But your friends have been great. I wouldn't want to hurt any of them."

Lexi hit the button for the garage door. While waiting for it to open, she studied Jack's profile. "You obviously caught the looks Travis was sending you."

"How could I miss them?" Jack chuckled, then sobered. "I understand where he was coming from. I wouldn't want him moving in with you."

His gaze met hers. Though the garage door was now fully opened, she made no move to pull the station wagon inside.

"I hope *you* understand why I can't offer my place," she said in a quiet tone. "It's not that I wouldn't enjoy having you around. It's just that—"

"It wouldn't be a good idea with a child in the house." Jack smiled at the look of surprise that flashed in her eyes. "What? You don't think I can be sensitive to all the nuances of this situation?"

"No, I—"

"You can't honestly think I care so little about you." Without Jack quite realizing how it had happened, the lighthearted teasing was gone, replaced by something deeper, something he didn't want to analyze too closely. He gave in to an impulse and touched her face. "I meant what I said the other day. I never want to do anything to hurt you or Addie."

She leaned her head into his caress and his heart filled with an emotion that was new, yet at the same time familiar.

"Mommy?" a sleepy voice sounded from the backseat.

Jack dropped his hand and pulled back.

"Are we home?" Addie straightened in the backseat, not bothering to cover her yawn.

"Yes, we are." Lexi pulled into the darkened garage and flicked off the ignition. "I should never have kept you out so late on a school night."

"'s okay, Mommy." Addie yawned again. "We don't have much going on tomorrow except for a math test."

Jack stifled a grin at Lexi's groan.

"I've got an idea." He twisted in his seat so he could see both Addie and Lexi. "How about I get up early and eat breakfast with Addie? That way I can help her review for the test before the school bus comes."

"Cool," Addie said, then a frown furrowed her brow. "Do you remember how to do fractions?"

"If I don't, you can teach me." Jack shot the girl a wink.

Addie giggled and shifted her gaze to her mother. "See, Mommy. It's going to be okay. Jack's going to help me study."

"I heard that." When Lexi shifted her gaze to meet his, the depth of emotion in her eyes surprised him. "Thank you."

Jack didn't understand the big deal. He certainly had the time. Besides, he liked Addie and wanted her to do her best on the test. And, after all Lexi had done for him, there wasn't anything he wouldn't do for her.

His heart skipped a beat when she reached over and gave his hand a squeeze.

No, there was nothing he wouldn't do for this woman.

"How's the undercover prince adjusting to life in Jackson Hole?" Rachel Milligan, the

E.R. nurse who'd been on duty when Jack had been brought in from Teton Village, gazed up at Lexi from the medication cart she was stocking.

"The prince is doing quite well." Lexi smiled, remembering the bet she'd made with the nurses the day Jack was brought into the E.R. "He sends his regards to the commoners at the hospital."

During most workdays, Lexi barely had a chance to catch her breath much less gossip with the staff. But this Friday the E.R. had been virtually deserted. That didn't happen very often. Lexi welcomed the break.

Rachel smiled then her expression turned serious. "By virtue of the fact that he's still in Jackson Hole, I take it he hasn't gotten his memory back."

Lexi leaned back against a counter that

smelled faintly of disinfectant. "Not yet. Hopefully his friends or family will come through."

Rachel's blonde brows pulled together. "I've been watching the paper and the Internet but I haven't seen a word about a Wyoming John Doe. Wasn't the Sheriff going to send out a press release?"

Lexi pressed her lips together. Jack had been right. His story hadn't stood a chance. "The press release already went out. Then the attack at the water treatment plant happened and—"

"—all the other stories got pushed aside." Rachel shook her head. "You know, I'm beginning to think if Jack Snow didn't have bad luck, he'd have no luck at all."

Lexi straightened. She pushed away from the counter. Her heart pounded against her ribs. "That's not true. Jack survived an avalanche that could have easily killed him. He's got a great place to live and friends who care about him."

"Lex, I'm sorry. I didn't mean to hit a nerve."

"You didn't. It's just sometimes when I think of what could have happened to him…" She took a deep breath and fought for control of her rioting emotions. "He *was* lucky. Very lucky."

Rachel's blue eyes softened. "He's fortunate to have you as a friend."

"You two are looking awfully serious." Dr. Wahl dropped into a chair behind the nurse's station.

"We were talking about Jack Snow and how lucky he is to have Lexi for a friend," Rachel said, ignoring the black look the social worker shot her.

"He's a good guy." David shifted his gaze to

Lexi. "July and I want to have you two over for dinner sometime."

"Sounds like you and the undercover prince are an item," Rachel teased.

David raised a brow. "Undercover prince?"

Lexi ignored the question. The doctors didn't need to know about the wagers the nurses had made. "I've been trying to expose Jack to new situations as much as possible. I'm hoping something he sees or hears will jog his memory."

"That's smart." David's gaze dropped to the PDA in his hand. He studied the screen for a long moment. "I don't think it'll be long."

Lexi's heart skipped a beat. "You really think Jack will regain his memory soon?"

David looked up and blinked. "I was referring to Mr. Brown in room five. His son and wife should be here shortly to pick him up."

"Of course," Lexi said, feeling her face warm. "I'll talk to them when they arrive and see if they have any needs."

"As far as Jack Snow goes, there's no way to predict how long it will take for him to remember his past," David said. "It could be today or tomorrow. It could be ten years from now."

Lexi's jaw dropped. "You told him the memory loss would be short-term."

"I said the vast majority are resolved in short order," David clarified. "But his best hope is that someone comes forth and identifies him."

Lexi exchanged a look with Rachel. Unless Jack got some newspaper or Internet exposure, the odds of someone identifying him weren't good. Not good at all.

Late the next week Lexi wheeled her car into a popular Jackson brewery's parking lot and pulled to a stop. "Are you sure you don't mind spending your Thursday night with a bunch of Hank and Mimi's relatives and friends?"

"I'm actually looking forward to it," Jack said. "So far I've liked all your friends. There shouldn't be any reason I won't like this group, as well."

Lexi bit her lip. How could she tell him that Mimi and Hank weren't exactly like her other friends? Perhaps it was best to let him meet them and make up his own mind.

Tonight's event was a belated engagement party for the betrothed couple. Hank had wanted the party to be held at Yellowstone. Mimi had wanted the Spring Gulch Country Club. With Lexi's nudging they'd compromised on a party room at a local brewery.

As a member of the wedding party, Lexi's presence was mandatory. If she was being honest she'd have to admit she'd been dreading the event. The maid of honor as well as the five other bridesmaids were all Mimi's friends from high school. Lexi had tried to get to know them, but they hadn't seemed interested in getting to know her in return.

While Lexi was also single, she was a mother. Almost a decade—and a world of experience—separated them. Somehow, whenever she was with them, she ended up feeling like a maiden aunt who wasn't all that interesting.

"Lexi?" Jack's touch on her arm pulled her from her reverie. "Would you prefer I not come?"

She shook her head and curved her fingers around his arm. "I want you to come with me. If you aren't there, who will I talk to?"

A look of confusion crossed his face. "I

thought you said all of Mimi and Hank's friends will be there."

"They will." Not wanting to diss Mimi or her friends, she chose her words carefully. "Mimi is only twenty-three. Her friends are also in their early twenties. While they're all very nice, we don't have a lot in common. Around them I feel old and well, stodgy."

Jack's cough sounded suspiciously like a laugh.

"I do," Lexi protested.

"Ah, Lexi." Jack shook his head and let his gaze linger. Although the party was casual, Lexi had dressed up her navy sweater with a beaded necklace. Her hair hung loose to her shoulders, the way he liked it. Old and stodgy? Not this lovely creature. "I've never seen Mimi. But there's no doubt in my mind that you, Miss

Stodgy, will be the most beautiful woman at this party."

Lexi's red lips tipped into a smile. "Have I ever told you how good you are for my ego?"

"Just being honest." Jack couldn't help giving her compliments. There was just so much about her he liked. So much about her that he… loved?

The thought brought a frown to his forehead. Love? No way. He couldn't be in love with her. Not possible. He'd only known her a couple weeks.

"Is something wrong?"

Jack brushed away the troublesome thought. He'd been looking forward to this evening ever since Lexi had invited him earlier in the week. Since Sarah and her parents would be heading home tomorrow, Addie was spending the night with her friend. That meant he and Lexi had the night to themselves.

"Everything is fine." He gazed into the most beautiful amber eyes he'd ever seen. "In fact, it couldn't be better."

"You are really super cute," Mimi said to Jack, her words coming out in a slur, her eyes glittery. "Have I told you that?"

"Only about a thousand times," Lexi said through gritted teeth. She pried Mimi's fingers from Jack's forearm. All evening Jack had done his best to keep his distance from the bride-to-be, but she wouldn't leave him alone. Lexi had finally had enough. "Hank is looking for you."

Mimi tilted her head. A look of confusion furrowed her brow. "Who?"

"Hank." Lexi somehow managed to keep a smile on her lips. "Your fiancé?"

"Oh, *Hank*." Mimi snorted. "I thought you said *tank*."

Apparently finding the thought incredibly funny, Mimi started laughing. Once she started, she didn't stop.

Lexi exchanged a look with Jack.

"Drunk," he mouthed.

Lexi nodded and with a resigned sigh turned back to the young woman who now had tears of laughter streaming down her cheeks.

"Mimi, this is your engagement party. Why don't you spend some time with your fiancé?" Lexi gestured to the other end of the bar where Hank stood drinking shots with a couple of his ranger buddies. "He looks lonely."

Mimi wiped the tears of laughter from her eyes and glanced in the direction Lexi had indicated. Something that looked almost like a snarl lifted her lips. "He cares more about animals and trees and drinking with his friends than he does about me."

Under the bitterness, Lexi swore she heard a hint of hurt in Mimi's voice. "I'm sure that's not true—"

"I want to go to Hawaii on my honeymoon. Everyone goes to Hawaii." Mimi's voice grew louder with each word. "But Mr. Park Ranger refuses to leave his precious park during high season."

Despite the noise in the room, Mimi's voice rang out above the din.

Hank slammed the shot glass on the bar and turned. His expression darkened and the glitter in his eyes told Lexi that Mimi wasn't the only one who'd had too much to drink this evening. "It's not just the job. We don't have the money to go to Hawaii," he bellowed. "You'd understand if you'd ever shut your mouth and listen."

The room took on a hushed chill.

Mimi didn't appear to notice. Her entire attention was now focused on her fiancé.

"I'm through listening to you, Hank. If you can't understand that a girl only gets married once, if you don't want to do everything in your power to make me happy, you're not the man for me." Mimi tugged the ring off her finger and threw it on the shiny mahogany bar. Then with a toss of her long blond hair, she flounced out of the room.

Lexi waited for Hank to follow. Instead he scooped up the ring and dropped it into his pocket. Then with a grim expression he turned back to his friends and downed another shot.

"Do you think I should go after her?" Lexi

asked Jack, who—like the rest of the room—had watched the scene unfold.

"If you think you should, then go. Don't worry about me." A thoughtful look settled on his face. "Though it might be a good idea to give Mimi some space. Throwing the ring at him was probably just an impulse. But this is the time for her to consider if she really wants this wedding to go on as scheduled. If Hank isn't the man she wants to spend the rest of her life with, it's best to end it now."

For the past several weeks Lexi had begun to have a bad feeling about Mimi and Hank's upcoming nuptials. The events tonight confirmed her worst fears. "You're right. If she and Hank are going to break up, it's better to do it before they walk down the aisle."

Jack frowned. "Otherwise he might leave her at the altar."

It was an odd comment. But then there was an odd look in Jack's eyes. As if he'd remembered something…

Lexi grabbed the sleeve of his sweater and pulled him into a little alcove, away from prying eyes and ears.

"If you want us to be alone, you just had to say the word," Jack teased, though the distant look remained in his brown eyes.

"You remembered something." She pinned him with her gaze. "What was it?"

"You know me too well," he said in a flip tone.

"Considering I don't even know your real name, I hardly think so." Lexi wasn't about to let him change the subject. "C'mon, spill."

Still he hesitated.

"Jack, you have to know by now that there's nothing you can't tell me." She leaned close, the clean, fresh scent she'd come to associate with him teasing her nostrils. "I won't judge you. But I can't help unless I know what's happening in that head of yours."

"I think—" he took a step back and raked a hand through his hair "—that I left someone at the altar."

When Lexi had been Addie's age, she'd fallen off her bicycle. She'd hit the ground so hard that all the air had been knocked from her lungs. She remembered that feeling. She felt the same way now.

However, underneath the shock and the breathlessness, joy sliced through her veins. *Jack isn't married. Jack isn't married. Jack isn't married.*

"You remember leaving a woman at the altar?" Lexi asked when she could finally speak again.

"I remembered the wedding," he said. "Just like before. But this time, I heard myself telling a guy in a tux that I couldn't do this. I needed to be absolutely sure she was the one for me before I took this step and I wasn't sure."

"What happened then?"

"I walked out of the church into the sunlight. I remember looking down at my left hand and being so happy there wasn't a wedding band on it. I liked Ellen. I cared about her. But I couldn't marry her."

"Ellen who?"

Jack blinked a couple of times. "Ellen?"

"You said 'I liked Ellen,'" Lexi reminded him. "What was Ellen's last name?"

Jack's brows pulled together in thought. After a long moment he shook his head.

"Where were you? Do you remember the state? The town?" Lexi pressed, though her heart had resumed beating the mantra *Jack isn't married, Jack isn't married.*

"I don't know." Jack rubbed a hand across his forehead. "That's all I remember. I know it's not much—"

"Not much? It's huge." Lexi grabbed his arm, her voice trembling with excitement. "Don't you realize the significance? You're not married. I, I mean we, don't have to feel guilty anymore about the kiss we shared."

A light flashed in his eyes. She saw the moment he made the connection because a smile lifted his lip. "That means it's also okay for me to do this—"

In a single heartbeat, he pulled her close and his lips covered hers. Lexi wrapped her arms around his neck and slid her fingers into his hair. Her mouth opened to his probing tongue and she lost herself in the sensations coursing through her body like an awakened river. This time there was no hesitation. On his side or on hers.

The chatter, the laughter, the chinking of glasses faded away. Lost in the kisses, she was barely conscious of him maneuvering them farther into the alcove, until she felt the wall behind her back. Still he continued to kiss her, long kisses that made her body ache with need and want.

His hand slipped under her sweater and skimmed up her side. Her breasts tingled with anticipation as his hand moved to the clasp of her bra.

Without warning his body slammed into hers.

"Watch where you're going," Jack growled as beer dribbled down his shoulder.

The burly outdoorsman who'd bumped into him stopped to survey the damage. He gave a snort of disgust at his now half-empty glass before shifting to Lexi. He appeared to take in her disheveled hair and swollen lips before dropping to Jack's proprietary hand on her waist. A smile split his lips before he chugged the last of the beer in his glass. Then he belched loudly. "You two should think about getting yourself a room."

Without another word he continued down the hall.

*Get a room.*

Jack met her gaze. "An interesting suggestion."

Lexi wasn't fooled by the casual tone. The heat in his eyes told her that the desire that held her in a stranglehold gripped him, too.

She'd never been into casual sex. At thirty-two, she'd only slept with two men—her high school boyfriend and Drew, Addie's father.

But what she felt for Jack was more than casual. She liked him. She admired him. And she wanted him with a passion that shocked her with its intensity. "No motel."

The light in his eyes dimmed but he didn't argue. "I understand. We haven't known each other—"

"It's not that." Lexi leaned forward and brushed her lips across his. "Addie's spending the night with Sarah."

His eyes never left her face. "Are you saying what I think you're saying?"

Lexi smiled. "There's absolutely no reason to spend money on a motel when we can sleep in my bed."

Jack's eyes gleamed. "I don't think either of us is going to get much sleep tonight."

Lexi smiled and kissed him again. "I hope not," she murmured against his lips. "That would be a waste of a perfectly fine bed."

## Chapter Ten

Jack had been inside Lexi's home once before. But he hadn't bothered to look around. This time, while she hung up their coats, he let his gaze linger.

The rustic cabin's interior was more spacious than the outside would suggest. A breakfast bar separated the kitchen from the living room. The fact that there were only two stools at the bar indicated that Lexi didn't do much entertaining. Though there were lots of homey touches—

pictures on the refrigerator and a hand-knitted throw on the chair—the tan leather sofa and the rest of the furniture matched the decor in the main lodge. The cabin might be her home, but it was clear she was still a guest.

"Would you like a glass of wine?" Lexi shut the door to the closet and turned.

The slight wobble to her voice resonated with him. It was as if they were two scared virgins about to make love for the first time. Of course he wasn't a virgin. At least he was *almost* positive he wasn't. And he wasn't scared. Well, maybe just a little. But only because he wanted to make tonight as special for her as she deserved. "I'd love a glass."

"Red?" She opened a cabinet and peered inside. "Or white?"

He moved to Lexi's side. Lifting one hand, he brushed her hair back from her face and planted a gentle kiss on her temple. "I want what you want."

Her breath caught. "White it is."

She retrieved the bottle and shimmied past him. "The corkscrew is in the top left-hand drawer. You can do the honors while I get the glasses."

Another man might have been discouraged by her going from hot to cold in sixty seconds. But in the past couple of weeks, Jack had gotten to know Lexi. It had been a long time since she'd had a man in her life, much less one in her bed. He wouldn't rush her.

After retrieving the corkscrew, Jack opened the bottle with ease. While she poured he glanced around the living room and found what he was looking for almost immediately. "Mind if I put on some music?"

Lexi looked up, the bottle of wine in her

hand. "There's a CD of piano concertos on top of the pile. Or you can pick something else from the stack."

He popped the CD into the stereo and dulcet piano tones filled the room. Lexi brought the wine into the room and carefully placed the bottle and half-filled glasses on the coffee table in front of the overstuffed sofa. But instead of taking a seat, she remained standing. It was almost as if she was trying to decide how best to proceed.

If tonight was all about him, he'd take her in his arms and make love to her now, on the sofa, on the floor, against the wall. To heck with wine and music and atmosphere. But this wasn't about him. This was about Lexi.

He eyed the unlit candles scattered throughout the room. "Do you have matches? The lighting in here seems a bit harsh."

"Candlelight and wine," she said in an exaggerated Southern drawl. She brought a hand to her chest, striking a pose. "Why, sir, if I didn't know better, I'd think you mean to seduce me."

Though Jack told himself to wait until everything was just perfect, he couldn't help himself. He had to kiss her. "Umm hmm," he murmured as his lips closed over hers. "Very soon."

The room took on a golden glow. While Lexi finished lighting the rest of the candles, Jack started a fire in the stone hearth.

She watched him survey the flames then drop down on the soft cushions, looking more handsome than any man had a right to look. When he called her name and patted the spot next to him, Lexi took a deep breath and reminded herself she could do this. It may have been eight years since a man had touched her intimately, but surely it was like riding a bike. And she'd always been good at riding. She sat beside him and offered a smile.

"A glass of wine, madame." He lifted her glass of Chardonnay from the coffee table and placed it in her hand. Then he sat back and slipped his arm around her shoulder.

For a second Lexi stiffened. She couldn't help herself. Thankfully, Jack didn't seem to notice. Or, if he did, he didn't comment. Instead he started asking her questions about Jackson Hole. When that topic was exhausted, he effortlessly sent the conversation in another direction.

She wasn't sure how long they sat there, sipping their wine, chatting about everything from current events to child-rearing techniques. The more they talked, the more Lexi realized that this guy had it all. He was intelligent, witty...

and sexy as hell. His spicy cologne teased her nostrils and she found herself focusing more on his lips than on his words.

His hair, which had been longish when he'd been found, now brushed his collar. Lexi's fingers itched to run through the wavy thickness and see if the hair was really as soft as it appeared.

Anticipation and excitement snuffed out the last flickers of hesitation. It was as if all the stars had aligned to grant her this night. Jack didn't have a wife. The fact that he'd recently left his fiancée meant he didn't even have a girlfriend. Her cabin was isolated, so no one needed to know he'd slept over. And with Addie spending the night with her friend, Lexi didn't have to worry about setting a bad example for her daughter.

Tonight wasn't about forever. It was about a

stark carnal hunger she hadn't even known she was capable of feeling.

Her gaze dropped to his arm, to the dark hair overlying the muscles beneath. Complaining of being hot, he'd shed his sweater about ten minutes ago leaving a dark T-shirt hugging his broad chest. She was seized with a sudden desire to run her hands over his body and feel the coiled strength of skin and muscle sliding under her fingers. She wanted him to touch her in the same way. She wanted to feel his hard body pressed against hers. She wanted to have him fill her—

"Condoms," she blurted out. "I'm not on the pill and I don't have any condoms."

He stopped midsentence and his lips quirked upward. "How you got from global warming to condoms, I don't think I want to know."

Color crept from her throat, heating her

cheeks. While he'd been discussing various methods of stabilizing greenhouse gas concentrations, she'd been mentally undressing him.

But he didn't seem upset by the interruption. In fact, a look of tenderness filled his gaze. "No worries. We have condoms. Lots of them, in fact."

"We do? I mean, you do?"

"I rode to Idaho Falls with one of the maintenance men this week," Jack said in an offhand tone. "While he was picking up something Coraline had special ordered, I stopped into a drugstore and did some shopping of my own."

Lexi didn't know whether to feel thankful or irritated. "So this was all planned?"

His eyes followed her sweeping gesture. "Of course not. But if anything did happen between us, I wanted to be prepared." There was concern in his eyes but not a hint of apology in his tone.

"It just seems so…calculated." She brushed a piece of lint from her dress and wondered why she was making a big deal about a good thing. Jack didn't become angry the way Drew used to when she'd questioned him. Instead he placed his wine glass on the coffee table and took her hand. He laced his fingers through hers, his thumb caressing her palm, sending heat shooting through her veins.

"From the moment I first met you, there's been this pull between us." His gaze never left hers. "A very strong pull."

There was a challenge in his eyes, as if he expected her to disagree. But how could she when he was only stating facts?

"That's true," she said slowly.

"I wanted you from the moment I first met

you." His fingers were not quite steady touching the curve of her cheek and trailed along the line of her jaw. "As things kept heating up between us, I wasn't sure how long we'd be able to hold out."

Lexi flung her arms around his neck. "I'm sorry," she whispered against his throat. "You were being the mature one. I don't know what got into me."

Tears sprang to her eyes but she blinked them back before he noticed.

"It's okay." His arm tightened around here. "That's what I like about our relationship. There's nothing we can't say to each other."

The warmth of his acceptance surrounded her like a favorite coat. She rested her head against her chest with a contented sigh. "I like that you're honest with me, Jack. And I like you…a lot."

"I feel the same." He planted a kiss on her hair, his heart beating strong and steady against her ear.

After a moment, Lexi slipped her hand under his shirt, her fingers playing with the belt buckle. "I think it would be a shame to let those condoms you bought go to waste."

"That same thought occurred to me," he whispered against her hair.

"Why don't you, ah, make yourself more comfortable?" She rose to her feet. "I'll freshen up and be back in a second."

He met her gaze, his eyes more black than brown in the dim light. "Don't be long."

Resisting the urge to sprint, Lexi strolled to her bedroom. Once there, she shrugged off her dress and undergarments in record time then jerked open a dresser drawer. She grimaced. The neatly folded flannel pj's and high-necked nightgowns seemed more suited to a nunnery than a night of passion.

She was ready to settle for shorts and a T-shirt when she saw Mimi's shower gift on the dresser. The lingerie shower, hosted by the maid-of-honor, was set for next week.

Lexi opened the unwrapped box and pushed aside the tissue. The ivory-colored negligee had caught her eye the moment she'd seen it in the store window. Though ivory was really more her color than Mimi's, she'd bought it anyway.

Seconds later, Lexi slipped the sheer fabric over her head. Before she left the room she took a moment to spritz on perfume. She didn't look in the mirror, afraid what she saw there might make her lose her nerve. But when she entered the living room she caught a glimpse of her reflection in the front window. Only then did she realize sheer was one thing, transparent quite another.

But the expression in Jack's eyes when he rose from the sofa, now clad only in boxers and a T-shirt, told her transparent was a very good thing.

"You're beautiful." His voice was a husky caress.

Suddenly Lexi no longer felt the urge to grab the throw she'd knitted from the chair and use it to cover her nakedness. Instead she walked straight to Jack and curled her fingers into the fabric of his shirt. "Is it just me or are you over-dressed?"

"Without you in the room, I was cold." Jack pulled her toward him, linking his arms lightly around her waist.

There was no space between them and

she could feel the hard length of his arousal against her.

"Are you still cold now?" she asked in a husky voice she barely recognized.

Jack's eyes glittered and he grinned. "Did someone turn on a blast furnace?"

Her chuckle turned to a gasp as he began trailing kisses down her neck.

Still he continued to kiss her, this time on the mouth. Long, passionate kisses that left her weak and trembling.

"You are so incredibly lovely," he murmured, easing her down to the rug in front to the fireplace. He kissed her with a slow thoroughness that made her tingle all the way to her toes before settling on the rug next to her. "I want to explore and taste every inch of your beautiful body."

She sat up and pulled the negligee over her head.

"I want to do the same." She cast a pointed glance at his T-shirt and boxers. "So those have to go."

His eyes shone in the candle's glow and his quicksilver smile sent her already heightened senses into overdrive. His shorts and shirt quickly joined her negligee on the floor.

Jack's gaze slowly surveyed her and the approval in his eyes made her bold.

"Do you like what you see?" she asked, batting her lashes.

"Very much." He planted a kiss on her lips that accelerated the heat flowing through her body.

He trailed a finger along her jawline and followed it with kisses. Then he dropped his gaze to her breasts. "I've wondered what you looked like."

"You've seen women before."

"Not you."

"Tell me what you like." He cradled her breasts in his wide palms, his thumbs teasing the sensitive tips. "Do you like this?"

She pressed her legs together as heat shot straight to her belly. "Oh, yes."

"How about this?" His mouth replaced where one hand had been.

His tongue slid around the nipple but kept stopping short of the tip. She laced her fingers through his hair, holding him to her, arching her back in a silent plea for more. She wanted to sob in frustration when he circled her nipple then once again moved away.

"Please," Lexi moaned.

She didn't need to ask twice. His mouth

closed over the aching tip. Pleasure shuddered through her as he drew the tight bud into the delicious heat of his mouth. Each erotic pull of his lips sent an answering pull deep in her belly.

When his hand slipped between her legs she moaned and squirmed beneath the pleasure of his touch. She was determined to make this last as long as possible. But it had been so long and he assaulted her senses on all fronts.

His lips. His tongue. His…fingers. Oh, God, those fingers played her like a fine violin, her desire rising like a crescendo. When he slipped one of those fingers inside her the orgasm she'd been trying to stave off struck. Delicate inner muscles contracted and she pressed herself against his hand, crying out.

He held her tight, kissing her face, her neck, her lips.

"I'm sorry," she said when she came back down to earth. "I wanted this to last forever and now it's over."

She couldn't keep the disappointment from her tone.

"Over?" Jack chuckled. His hand flattened against her lower back, drawing her up against the length of his body. "Sweetheart, that was just the appetizer."

Lexi awoke the next morning to find Jack's head beside hers on the pillow. Even with his hair tousled against his cheeks and a five o'clock shadow darkening his jaw, he looked magnificent.

Her mouth curved into an almost feline smile. She'd never thought of herself as a woman of deep passions, but last night Jack had shown her how little she knew herself. It had been a most amazing night. He'd taken her to places she'd never thought possible, but she'd willingly gone because she trusted him. He hadn't let her down. Last night they hadn't just had sex, they'd made love. Though he hadn't said the words, she could see he cared, in his eyes, in his touch. The emotion between them had taken the physical to a whole other level.

Although Lexi was no virgin, last night had felt like the first time. There was a bond between her and Jack, an intimacy that made what she'd experienced before pale in comparison.

"I love you," she whispered, brushing the hair back from his face with a gentle hand.

He stirred but didn't open his eyes.

"I love you, too," he murmured.

A wave of contentment washed over Lexi. She laid her head on the pillow and snuggled against him. After years of telling herself that she didn't need a man in her life, she'd broken her own rule. In only a few short weeks she'd fallen in love. Not only that, she'd fallen in love with a man who didn't know his own name.

## *Chapter Eleven*

It was standing room only at the The Coffee Pot Café in downtown Jackson. Still Jack opened the door and followed Lexi and Addie inside. He found his gaze lingering on the families waiting for a table. What would it be like to be a family man? To wake up next to the woman you loved every morning and go to bed with her every night? To nurture a child to adulthood? At this moment he couldn't imagine anything better. Especially if his family was the woman and child at his side.

"Looks like it's going to be a while," Lexi said.

"I'm hungry," Addie whined.

"We can try someplace else," Jack said. "How about—"

"Mrs. Vaughn is waving to us." Addie tugged on his hand and pointed. "See. Over there."

Lexi narrowed her gaze. "It looks like they have empty seats at their table."

"I want to sit by Connor." Addie started forward but Lexi grabbed her hand and cast Jack a questioning look.

"Are you okay with us joining them?" she asked in a low tone.

"Please, Jack," Addie begged.

Jack grinned. "Of course. I like your friends."

"They're your friends, too," she reminded him.

Lexi released her hold on her daughter and Addie ran on ahead. Jack followed Lexi to the back of the café, resting his hand on the small of her back as they wove their way through the tables. It felt good to touch her. To be here with her.

He dropped his hand when they reached the table and pulled out her chair. Apparently they'd just missed David, July and baby Adam.

Jack recognized Lexi's friends—Mary Karen and her three boys, John and Kayla Simpson and Emma. Rachel Milligan, the nurse who'd tended to him in the E.R., sat visiting with Mary Karen at the far end of the table. The only person Jack didn't know was the older gentleman seated next to Kayla, across the table from him.

Jack stretched his hand out to the gray-haired

man. "I don't believe we've met. I'm Jack Snow, a friend of Lexi's."

*Friend* didn't seem a strong enough word considering what they'd shared last night, but it had to do.

"Al Dugan," the man said, giving Jack's hand a firm shake. "I'm Kayla's father. I'm in town for a visit."

As he took his seat Jack caught Lexi's concerned glance. He shot her a reassuring wink. She didn't need to worry about entertaining him.

"Since you're visiting, I take it you don't live in Jackson Hole," Jack said to the older man.

"I did until fifteen years ago. That's when I accepted a promotion and moved to Billings." The gray-haired gentleman took a sip of coffee and Jack could tell the old guy was just getting warmed up. "I was already divorced from Kayla's mother by then. Kayla was in high school and caught up in her activities, so there was really nothing keeping me here."

"Did you ever remarry?" Jack asked, not sure why he was so curious about the man's personal life.

Al shook his head. "The job took all my free time. My coworkers became my family and work became my life." The man's gaze turned sharp and assessing. "You got kids, Jack?"

*I don't think so.*

"No," Jack said. "No wife. No kids."

"Are you a career man?"

Jack shrugged, not sure how to answer that one.

"Looking back, I gave the job too much and my daughter too little." Al paused for a long moment. "You know, on the day I retired my boss didn't even come to my luncheon. Can you believe it?"

Hurt and anger underscored the man's words. Jack was happy when the food came and the talk shifted to sports. Still he couldn't help wondering if the man was angry with his employer…or with himself.

"I'm sorry about that." Lexi slanted a sideways glance at Jack as they walked to the Suburu. Addie skipped down the sidewalk in front of them. "Mary Karen and Kayla were in a talkative mood, but I shouldn't have left you to fend for yourself."

"No worries." Jack shot her a reassuring smile. "Just sitting beside you was enough for me. I kept imagining you naked."

He lowered his voice, the last words for her ears only.

Color flooded her face in a warm tide. Lexi didn't even have to close her eyes to remember how they'd barely settled on the mattress when he'd touched her. Sleep suddenly had been the furthest thing from her mind—

"Mommy, can Jack come with us? Pretty, pretty please?"

Addie's plea pulled Lexi from her reverie. She blinked, her heart still fluttering. The desire she'd thought had been satiated last night was back, stronger than ever. "Umm, what?"

She made the mistake of glancing at Jack. The heat in his eyes told her she wasn't the only one who wanted more…

"Please, Mommy. Can he come with us?" Addie repeated.

Lexi shifted her attention back to her daughter. "Come where?"

"Family day at the Y." Addie's brows pulled together. "You didn't forget, did you?"

Lexi saw the worry in her daughter's eyes. Though she had forgotten all about the event Addie had been anticipating for weeks, she shot her little girl a reassuring smile and lied through her teeth. "Me, forget? No way. I thought we'd stop at home, change our clothes and head straight to the gym."

"Family day?" Jack asked.

"It's an event the YMCA holds every April," Lexi explained as she clicked open the doors to the SUV with the remote. "And you're invited."

Lexi didn't want Jack to feel obligated, but she found herself hoping he'd say yes. "There are lots of activities for parents and children as well as booths filled with games of chance like you'd see at a carnival."

"'N' cotton candy," Addie added as if to

sweeten the deal. "Lots and lots of cotton candy."

"Do you like cotton candy?" Lexi asked him.

"I don't know," Jack said. "But I think this is a good time to find out."

"It's yummy, isn't it?" Addie stuffed a big wad of rainbow-colored cotton candy into her mouth.

Jack took another bite of the spun sugar. "Very yummy."

Lexi had stepped outside to take a call from the hospital, leaving Jack in charge of Addie.

"What happened to your little friends?" Since they'd first stepped into the noisy gymnasium, Addie had been surrounded by a whole gaggle of giggling girls.

Addie dropped her gaze to the cotton candy

and her smile faded. "They're with their daddies getting ready for the bean-bag relay."

"That sounds like fun."

"I guess." Addie lifted one small shoulder in a slight shrug. "I have a daddy. But he's not here today."

What Lexi had told him about Addie's father could be summed up in two words—*not much.* Jack was fairly certain the guy wasn't involved and didn't live in Wyoming, but he decided to play dumb. "Does your dad live around here?"

"He lives far away. He doesn't like me." Tears filled the child's amber eyes. "Even if he was here, he probably wouldn't want to do the relay with me."

Jack's heart clenched. He wanted to gather the girl in his arms and assure her that wasn't true. Instead he held out his hand as the dads and daughters moved to the middle of the gym for the start of the relays. "Want to climb to the top of the bleachers with me?" he asked. "I bet it's really cool up there."

Addie looked at him and blinked. Then, with an expression of trust, she slipped her hand in his.

The feel of that small little hand brought a lump to his throat. After climbing hand in hand to the very top plank, they took a seat far from the other spectators. For several minutes they watched the elementary-aged girls and their dads taking turns running then tossing a bean bag through a wooden bear's open mouth. Addie heaved a sigh that seemed much too heavy for a seven-year-old.

Jack took a long sip of his cola. "What makes you think your dad doesn't like you?"

"He just doesn't." Addie shrugged again, her lips turning down like a sad little clown. At that moment, he'd have given anything to see her twirl and giggle.

"Have you ever met him?"

"No."

Jack released the breath he didn't realize he'd been holding. *So far so good.* "Before I came to Jackson, I didn't like or dislike you because I didn't know you."

Addie cocked her head and he could almost see her mind processing his words.

"Now that I *do* know you, I like you," Jack continued. "You're smart and funny and nice. I'm positive anyone who met you would feel the same way."

"Even my daddy?"

The bald hope in her eyes tugged at his heartstrings. Jack cursed the man who didn't have enough sense to know what he'd given up.

"Yep." Jack gave a decisive nod. "Even your dad."

Without warning Addie flung her arms around his neck, squeezing tight. "I wish you were my daddy."

"I wish I was, too, sweetie." A lump rose to Jack's throat. The man was a fool. "I wish I was, too."

After concluding her phone conversation, Lexi returned to the gym.

"Have you seen Jack and Addie?" she asked Mary Karen, who was working in the face-painting station.

Mary Karen glanced up from the pink butterfly wings she was painting on a little girl's cheeks. "You might want to check with Rachel. She's manning the first-aid station and has a better view of the entire gym."

"I'll do that." Lexi wasn't too concerned. She knew wherever they were Jack was taking good care of her daughter. "Talk to you later."

"Hey, Lex," Mary Karen called when she turned to leave.

Lexi turned and lifted a brow.

"What's it like having a guy around?" Mary Karen asked. "Is it…weird?"

Startled by the unexpected question, Lexi didn't answer for a second. Then she smiled. "It's nice," she said. "In fact, I'd highly recommend it."

Then, with a wave, she went in search of her missing daughter and her friend, er, boyfriend?

She found the two sitting companionably at the top of the bleachers. The fact that she was out of breath when she reached them told her she needed to get back to the gym…and pronto. "What are you guys doing way up here?"

"Talking about my daddy," Addie said in a matter-of-fact tone. "Jack said if my daddy met me, he'd like me. Do you think he would?"

Lexi took a deep breath. She'd never tried to keep Addie from talking about her father, but she couldn't remember the last time her daughter had mentioned him. "Of course he'd like you, sweetheart."

"Addie thought her dad didn't like her," Jack said in a light tone, though his eyes were serious. "I told her if he met her, he'd like her. How could he not? She's a great little girl."

Addie smiled, and he could tell his words had pleased her. She glanced down at the gymnasium floor, to the main stage area where a family of cloggers bowed to the crowd. "My cheer team is up next. Are you and Jack gonna watch me?"

"Wouldn't miss it," Jack said.

"I'll definitely be watching," Lexi promised her daughter.

Addie started down the steps then paused. "Will you still be up here when I get done?"

"We'll be right here." Without warning Jack's hand clasped Lexi's. "I've got your mom in my clutches and I'm not going to let her go."

The vow, delivered in a monster voice worthy of Count Dracula, made Addie giggle. "You're silly."

Lexi waited until her daughter was out of earshot before she turned to Jack. "Okay, what was that about her father?"

"Apparently the dad-and-daughter relay race got her thinking about her father," he said. "She told me her dad didn't like her. You heard what I told her."

"Thank you for that," she said. "I'm just surprised it came up."

"I'm not," he said. "When my mom took off, for years I thought it was my fault. But I never said anything to my dad."

He paused as if realizing the significance of what he'd said.

"Your mother deserted you?" she said in as casual of a tone as she could muster.

Jack nodded, seeming lost in the memory. "I was five. From then on it was just me and him."

"You must have been very close."

Jack tilted his head. "I don't…remember."

"It's okay." Lexi tightened her fingers around his. "Pretty soon all your memories will return and you'll be back with your family."

The realization was like a stake to her heart.

"I'm not worried about it," he said. "I'm very comfortable with the way things are right now."

"What about money?" she asked. "Your cash has to be running out."

"It's gone." He shook his head but a smile still hovered on his lips. "That's why I accepted Coraline's offer to help out around the lodge in exchange for room and board."

Lexi felt her spirits lift. "You won't have to move in with Mary Karen."

"I wouldn't have moved in with her anyway."

Lexi ignored her heart's flutter and pointed to the stage on the gym floor. "Addie's junior cheer squad is getting ready to perform."

Jack's gaze never left her face. "We should start dating."

"Isn't that what we've been doing?"

"We've been spending time together," he said pointedly. "The social worker helping the guy with amnesia. I want more. I want to be part of a couple…with you."

The way her heart was beating you'd have thought she was fifteen and he'd asked her to go steady. She tried to remember why she'd thought dating was a bad idea. "I don't want Addie to—"

"—know that her mom could care about a man?"

Said that way, her reservations did sound a bit silly. Still, there had to be ground rules. "You couldn't sleep over."

"I understand that," Jack said. "But I bet we could find other times to be alone." He trailed a finger up her arm. "Other times and other ways that I could show you how much you mean to me."

"It's just so hard—"

He tipped her chin up with his fingers and gazed into her eyes. "What is?"

Lexi swallowed hard. "You could be gone tomorrow."

"There are many unknowns in life." His hand

tightened around hers. "That's why we have to enjoy the time we've been given."

It made sense. Still, Lexi hesitated. "I'm scared, Jack. In fact I'm terrified you'll remember your previous life, leave and never look back."

"Ah, Lex." He draped an arm over her shoulder. "You don't have to worry. The way I feel about you, I can't imagine ever leaving you— or Addie—behind."

The way he felt? Her heart skipped a beat. Could he have meant those words he'd murmured to her last night?

"Are you willing to give us a shot?"

Lexi brought a finger to her lips and pretended to think. But she couldn't keep the smile from her lips. "What do I have to lose?"

He kept his arm around her shoulders while they watched Addie perform. Being with him felt so right. And she'd spoken the truth. She didn't have anything to lose. She'd already given him her heart. All she could hope now was that he took good care of it.

"Are you sure you wouldn't rather eat in the lodge?" Lexi glanced at Jack as she placed the pizza she'd taken from the oven on the counter of the breakfast bar. "Coraline usually makes Swiss steak on Saturday night."

"Swiss steak, yuck." Addie wrinkled her nose. "I'd rather have pizza."

"I'd rather have dinner with the two of you," Jack said with a gallantry that warmed her heart.

"Well, we're happy to have you," Lexi said. "If you could pour the drinks while I cut the pizza, we should be ready to eat."

Jack opened the refrigerator door, reached inside and grabbed a liter of soda.

"Jack," Lexi said in a hushed tone.

He shifted his gaze.

"Milk," she mouthed.

*Of course. A growing girl needs milk, not soda.*

Jack put the soda down, grabbed a carton of milk instead and filled three glasses.

Addie stared at hers. "I want soda."

"I like milk," Jack declared. Before Lexi could respond to her daughter's whine, he took a big sip. "Yum. Nice and cold, just the way I like it. Is yours cold, too, Addie?"

Addie picked up her glass with both hands and took a drink. "Very cold."

Lexi smiled her approval. "After dinner, it's movie night. Addie chose *Bambi.*"

"Bambi?"

"Bambi is a deer," Addie explained, her young face earnest. "And Thumper is his friend. Thumper is a rabbit."

"I know you said you had time for pizza, but I don't remember if you had something else planned for later tonight?" Lexi said.

She was giving him an out. Jack took another sip of milk. It wasn't really too bad. In fact, given time he might acquire a taste for the white stuff.

"Jack?"

Yes, she was giving him an out, but it was one he didn't want to take. He wanted to spend the evening with his girls. If that meant watching a movie about the adventures of a deer and a rabbit, that's what he was going to do.

Addie fell asleep before the movie ended, wedged between him and Lexi on the sofa.

"I'll carry her into the bedroom and you can take it from there," Jack whispered.

"Works for me." Lexi stood and stretched. "Addie's getting so big it's getting hard for me to carry her."

"Another reason for having a man around." Jack scooped the child up into his arms. When they reached her bed, he carefully placed her on the top of the covers then impulsively brushed a kiss on her hair. "Sleep tight, little one."

He straightened to find Lexi staring. "Something the matter?"

"I was just thinking how much Addie's missed by not having a father around." Her gaze grew distant and he knew she was thinking about the ex-boyfriend who'd deserted her.

"You realize that a guy doesn't have to be a child's biological father to be her dad." His tone was light but his expression was serious.

Lexi met his gaze and smiled. "I'm beginning to see that."

"If you need me for anything, I'll be in the other room." He grinned. "I have to see how the movie ends."

## Chapter Twelve

"You know all work and no play makes Ellen—"

"—a dull girl." Ellen didn't have to look up from her computer screen to know who'd opened her office door. For the past two weeks Steve had continued to stop by her office on his way out the door. Every night he asked her to go to dinner with him. Every night she turned him down.

The one time she had gone out with him,

they'd laughed and talked until almost two. When she'd gone to bed that night, it had been Steve, not Nick, who'd filled her dreams. That's when she'd come to her senses. She was almost engaged to Nick. That meant she shouldn't be seeing other men. Period. End of story.

"I was going to stop by Hanabi tonight." The tall attorney ambled into the room and took a seat. "I thought we could eat then get started on the Thompson case over dinner."

Ellen's refusal died in her throat. She hadn't had sushi since last summer when she and Steve used to stop by Hanabi at least once a week. After she'd started dating Nick, she'd tried to get him to go with her a couple of times. But Nick was a meat and potatoes kind of guy. A true Texan. Steve, well, surprisingly the former football player liked the bluefin tuna almost as much as she did.

Ellen leaned back in her chair and felt her heart pick up speed. It sounded like tonight would be business, not social. "The Thompson case?"

"I can fill you in over dinner."

"Let me sign off." Ellen had planned to surf the Internet and see if she could track Nick down. It had been over three weeks since he'd taken off. Though his father still wasn't concerned, Ellen worried.

"Is something the matter?" Steve leaned over the desk, his eyes filled with concern. "If tonight doesn't work for you we—"

"It's fine." Ellen inhaled the tantalizing scent of his cologne. "I had something else I was going to do, but it can wait. It's not that important."

The next week passed swiftly. Jack spent every spare minute with Lexi and Addie. He and Lexi had become a couple in the eyes of the community. He'd worried Addie might be jealous since she'd had her mom to herself all these years, but she'd accepted him into their little family with a maturity that amazed him.

Still, he and Lexi kept displays of affection in front of her to hand-holding and a kiss on the cheek. And he didn't spend the night.

Today he'd finished his chores around the lodge and had caught a ride with the van driver into town. It had been exactly a month since he'd first met Lexi and he wanted to surprise her for lunch. He knew she didn't have plans because she'd told him she'd be using the time to go through her mail and do her bills.

He was banking on the fact that the bills could wait until tonight. After checking on her whereabouts with the hospital receptionist, he headed to the emergency room. She was just coming out of a room when he got there. His heart flip-flopped when he saw her. "Hello, beautiful."

"Jack." Her lips widened into a welcoming smile before worry filled her gaze. "Is everything okay?"

"Everything is wonderful. The sun is shining. The temperature is supposed to hit seventy today. And I'm here to take my best girl to lunch. That is, if you're available?"

"I am," she said. "Except we'll have to eat in the cafeteria."

"Works for me."

A doctor in a white lab coat followed by a nurse emerged from one of the exam rooms. It amazed Jack that less than a month ago these two were strangers to him. Now they were friends. "David. Rachel."

"What brings you by the hospital today?"

David cast a sideways glance at Lexi. "As if I didn't know."

"I came by to take Lexi to lunch."

"That's sweet." Rachel smiled. "Where are you going?"

"We're eating in the hospital cafeteria," Lexi said.

"Oh," David said. "Good luck to you."

"I heard a rumor that you're the new handyman at Wildwoods," Rachel said.

"It's true," Jack said. "My money ran out and Coraline was gracious enough to allow me to work for my room and board."

"What does she have you doing?" Rachel asked.

"Changing lightbulbs, keeping the parking lot and the common areas clean, stuff like that." Jack didn't feel challenged by the work, but he wasn't about to complain.

"I bet you're hoping you remember who you are soon," Rachel said. "Or that a family member or friend shows up to ID you."

"I saw they ran your story again in the Jackson Hole News," David said. "It was a nice article. I'm sure the wire services are all over it."

"The nurses upstairs were saying they saw the story on a couple of Internet sites." Lexi's expression gave nothing away.

"Well, so far no phone calls." Jack wished they were alone so that he could reassure Lexi again that whoever he was before didn't matter. "The sheriff said he'd call if he got any response."

Lexi glanced down at her watch. "I have a meeting with a family of an intensive-care patient at two, so if we're having lunch we better go now."

Though Jack couldn't put his finger on it, there was something different about Lexi today. Something was troubling her but he couldn't tell if it was work-related or personal. He tried to take her hand on their walk to the cafeteria, but she pretended not to notice.

A rock settled in the pit of his stomach. This had to be related to the conversation in the E.R. Though the last thing he wanted to bring up over lunch was the possibility of him leaving, once they'd sat down with the food, he didn't see that he had a choice. "Finding out who I am isn't going to change how I feel about you."

"I know you think that." Lexi dipped her spoon into the yogurt but made no attempt to pull it out. Instead she leaned forward, resting both her arms on the table, her expression earnest. "What if your family doesn't like me? Or like the fact that I have a child and have never been married?"

"All that matters are our feelings." This wasn't the first time they'd had this conversation. But he was willing to have it a hundred times a day if it would allay her fears.

A smile lifted her lips. "You're right. I don't know why I feel so anxious. Maybe it's because my day started off badly and I've had this uneasy feeling, like I was waiting for the other shoe to drop."

"What happened this morning?" he asked, curious but not overly concerned. If it had something to do with Addie, he knew Lexi would have called him.

"Mimi called," she said. "From Hawaii."

Jack cocked his head. "Mimi? As in Hank and Mimi?"

"The same. Except there is no more Hank

and Mimi." Lexi's lips twisted. "Now it's Mimi and Kyle."

Jack straightened in his chair. "Who's Kyle?"

"Her Pilates instructor," Lexi said. "They eloped."

"Wow." Jack wasn't sure how to respond. After all, Mimi was Lexi's friend. He took a sip of iced tea. "How did Hank take the news?"

"Apparently he went out and got drunk with his buddies."

"I bet you're disappointed that you don't get to wear that gorgeous bridesmaid's dress."

Lexi laughed. "Yeah, I'm crushed."

"It's not all bad," Jack said, trying to find the silver lining. "At least she'll get the flower deposit back."

"She made me take out the clause," Lexi said. "So now she—or rather she and Kyle—will have to pay all that money for flowers she'll never use."

Jack shook his head. "You put in so much work on her wedding."

"And it's not over yet," Lexi said with a rueful smile. "She asked me to forward her mail to her."

"Forward her mail?"

"She and Hank were looking for a place to live once they married. Apparently his current apartment didn't meet her high standards." Lexi rolled her eyes. "Because she was in such a state of transition—her words, not mine—she gave the wedding vendors my address. I can tell you I'm getting rid of those suckers right away. In fact…"

Lexi's gaze dropped to her purse. She reached inside her large bag and pulled out a small stack of envelopes. "I bet some of these are hers."

Jack took a bite of hamburger and chewed while Lexi flipped through the stack. She stopped and an odd look crossed her face. "The return address on this envelope is a law firm in Columbus, Ohio."

"Does Mimi know someone in Ohio?"

"No, but I do." Lexi lifted her gaze to meet his. "That's where Addie's dad lives."

"Didn't you tell me you'd asked him to relinquish all claim to her?" Jack said in a matter-of-fact tone. He didn't like seeing Lexi so upset over something that was probably nothing. "I bet he had an attorney draw something up and send it to you."

"You're probably right."

"I know I'm right. Open it and see."

"Lexi Brennan, report to intensive care. Lexi Brennan, please report to intensive care immediately," the voice over the loudspeaker said in a monotone.

Lexi heaved a sigh and rose to her feet.

"Aren't you going to open it?"

"No time." Lexi dropped the envelopes back into her bag. "Looks like my two o'clock appointment came early. I'll open it when I get home. I'm sure you're right. It's probably nothing."

When Jack got to Lexi's house shortly before six, he expected to see the grill fired up and ready for the steaks he'd brought over. Thankfully Lexi liked red meat as much as he did. But the grill cover was still on and the deck was deserted.

He knocked on the door, wondering if somehow they'd gotten their signals crossed. "Lexi. Addie."

The door slowly opened and Addie peered around it. "Shh." The child brought a small finger to her lips. "We have to be quiet. Mommy doesn't feel good."

Jack stepped inside the silent, dark house. "What's the matter?"

He kept his voice casual and offhand, not wanting to worry Addie. But he was worried. Lexi had been fine at lunch.

"She has a migraine." Addie's brows drew together. "And maybe her tummy hurts, too."

"I'm going to see how she's doing." He handed the steaks wrapped in butcher paper to Addie. "Could you put these in the refrigerator for me?"

Addie nodded solemnly. She started toward the kitchen then turned back. "Mommy is going to be okay, isn't she?"

"She's going to be just fine." But even as Jack

hurried down the hall, an uneasy feeling slithered up his spine. As his hand closed over the
doorknob to her room, he found himself pray-
ing that whatever was wrong was something
that could be easily fixed.

Lexi knew she needed to get up and make
Addie some dinner, but she couldn't make her
limbs move. Instead she lay on her bed in pitch
darkness staring up at the ceiling, her head
pounding.

She'd worried that this day would come, but
had never *really* believed it would. For someone who prided herself on addressing every
issue head-on, this time she felt like pulling
the covers over her head in the hopes that it
would go away.

She heard the door open. "I'll be up and make
you something to eat in a minute, sweetheart."

"Are you okay? Is there anything I can get you?"

*Jack.* She'd forgotten they'd made plans to grill out.

"I forgot to call you." Tears welled up in her eyes and filled her voice. "That wasn't very nice."

"Don't cry." He sat on the bed and brushed the tears from her cheeks with the pads of his thumbs. "Tell me what's wrong."

"It's just a migraine," she murmured, the meds making her tongue thick and clumsy in her mouth. "I haven't had one in a long time. It's partially hormonal, mostly stress."

"Was it this thing with Mimi?" he asked. "Is that what brought this on?"

Lexi choked back a hysterical giggle. "Mimi is the least of my worries."

"What can I do to make it better?"

"There's nothing you can do," Lexi said, welcoming the inky darkness that was rapidly closing over her. "I'm afraid there's nothing anyone can do."

## Chapter Thirteen

*There's nothing anyone can do.*

The words played over and over in Jack's mind. While Lexi slept, he and Addie ate a simple dinner of grilled cheese sandwiches, tomato soup and a big glass of milk.

After dinner he helped Addie with her homework, said prayers with her at bedside and then tucked her in. When he returned to the living room he tried to watch television but found it difficult to concentrate. Despite knowing she needed her sleep, he was seriously tempted to wake Lexi. He didn't like it that she was distressed yet he didn't know enough to be able to fix whatever bothered her.

Opening the refrigerator door, Jack pulled out the cola he'd been craving since he'd walked through the door. He'd barely taken a sip when he heard a bedroom door open. His lips lifted in a wry smile. It figured Addie would get up just when he'd grabbed a soda.

He turned, hiding the can behind his back. But it wasn't Addie who ambled into the room but a very rumpled Lexi. She'd changed into an obviously much loved pair of sweatpants and a long-sleeved green shirt that didn't show any skin. Her dark hair stuck out in the back and there was a criss-cross pattern on her cheek from a blanket. But when her eyes brightened and a smile lifted her lips, Jack's heart answered with a rush of love.

"How are you feeling?" he asked.

"Better." She rubbed the back of her neck with one hand. "The headache is almost gone." She glanced around the room. "Where's Addie?"

"In bed."

"So early?"

"It's after nine."

Alarm skittered across Lexi's face. "Ohmigosh, she has to be starving."

When she turned toward the girl's bedroom, Jack touched her arm. "Relax. She's already eaten."

Confusion blanketed Lexi's face. "But how?"

"I may not have a memory, but I am not without talent." Jack shot her a wink. "We had soup and a sandwich and milk. Lots and lots of milk."

The tenseness which had gripped Lexi's shoulders eased. "Thank you."

"It was no trouble." Jack waved a dismissive hand. "She's a nice little girl. You've done a good job raising her."

Lexi thought about the letter and a wave of despair washed over her. "That may not matter."

Jack sat his soda on the table, took her hand and led her to the sofa. Once she'd sat down, he took a seat beside her.

"Tell me what's wrong." His warm brown eyes invited confidences.

Lexi's gaze drifted to the side table where her purse sat, the letter peeking out from the side pocket. It was hard to believe that one minute everything could be wonderful and the next…

She shuddered and swallowed the sob that rose to her throat.

Jack's arm closed around her shoulder. He tugged her close. "Talk to me, sweetheart. I can't help if I don't know what's wrong."

How long had it been since she'd had some-one to lean on? Someone to share her burdens? Ever since her father had died she'd been on her own. Lexi brushed the tears from her cheeks with the pads of her fingertips. "There's noth-ing you—or I—can do. Drew has money on his side."

"Drew? Your ex?" Jack's gaze turned sharp and assessing.

Lexi took a deep breath. "Remember when I told you I'd written to him several months ago asking him to relinquish all claim to Addie and he hadn't written back?"

A knowing look filled his eyes. "Is this about the letter you received from the law firm in Ohio?"

Not trusting her voice, Lexi pressed her lips together and nodded. Her emotions were raw. If they were any closer to the surface she'd be bleeding.

"So he's not interested in your proposal," Jack said. "That's okay. It doesn't change anything."

"He wants custody of Addie," Lexi blurted out.

The shock on Jack's face would have been funny at any other time. "Beg pardon?"

"Apparently Drew has decided he wants to be a dad after all." To Lexi's surprise, though she was quaking inside, her voice didn't waver. "He's got the money to make that happen."

"He's been out of her life since she was born." After his initial surprise, Jack didn't seem all that concerned. "That won't look good to the court. Has he been paying child support?"

Lexi shook her head. "He never offered. I never asked."

"That's another black mark against him." Jack met her gaze. "May I see the letter?"

"Of course." Lexi jumped up but stilled when the room spun. She waited, giving the room a chance to right itself. "The pills make me a little dizzy."

"You sit back down." He rose and put his arm around her waist. "Tell me where it is and I'll get it."

"It's in my purse." Lexi gestured with a flick of her head. "It's that piece of paper sticking out of the side pocket."

Though she tried for matter-of-fact, the tremble in her voice gave her away.

Jack pulled her closer to him. "This will be okay."

"I wish I shared your optimism." Her attempt

at a laugh fell flat. She disentangled herself from his arms and collapsed onto the soft cushions.

When Jack crossed the room to get the letter, Lexi rested her head against the back of the sofa and closed her eyes. If only she could go to sleep and wake up to find this had only been a bad dream.

"While I'm up can I get you something to eat or drink?"

Lexi slowly opened her eyes.

"Piece of toast? Some crackers?"

"I'm not all that hungry." She rubbed a hand across her face, incredibly weary. "Could you bring the letter over here? I'd like to read it again."

"You're the client," he said, then paused. "I mean, it's your letter."

Jack returned to the sofa, but only after pulling a sleeve of soda crackers from a drawer in the kitchen. He settled beside her and handed her the crackers. "Even if you don't feel like eating, I want you to try at least one," he said softly. "Please."

Lexi pulled a couple of squares from the already opened sleeve. "If it will make you happy, I'll do it."

He responded to her teasing tone with a brilliant smile. "It makes me happy. *You* make me happy."

She smiled and took a bite of cracker.

As if satisfied, Jack's gaze dropped to the letter in his hand.

Lexi's heart clenched as he unfolded the vellum sheet and began to read. She dropped her gaze to the paper and followed along. But she really didn't need to read it again. She'd reviewed it so many times she had each word memorized.

Jack's lips tipped upward when he was about two-thirds of the way through the letter. She couldn't figure out what he found so amusing in a letter that threatened to rock her world.

"No worries." His gaze lifted. "This letter is nothing more than an intimidation tactic."

He made it sound like that was a good thing. Lexi's spirits cautiously rose. "I don't understand."

"By sending this to you on a law firm's stationary, they're trying to throw their weight around and make you believe you're at their mercy. The truth is you're in control."

He sounded so confident, so certain. Still…

"Are you telling me Drew doesn't have a leg to stand on?" The fear that had gripped her since she'd first read the letter began to ease.

"I wouldn't exactly say that." Jack's businesslike tone softened at her sound of distress. "He is Addie's father. And by writing the letter and making that request you, in essence, established paternity."

"Are you saying this is my fault?" Lexi jumped to her feet, her headache flaring. "That I'm going to lose my daughter because of a stupid letter I wrote?"

The mere thought that something she did could result in Addie having to live with a man who never wanted her to be born broke Lexi's heart…and made her angry.

"Sweetheart." He kept trying to put his hand on her, and she kept turning.

"Why does it have to be like this?" She pressed her lips together, fighting tears. "Why didn't I leave well enough alone?"

He put both arms out, corralling her movements until she folded into him against her will and he held her. "Lexi, darling, none of this is your fault. None of it."

She clung to him, feeling her anger subside. She took a deep, steadying breath. "Tell me how to fight this. I'm not giving Addie to that man."

"It's hard to say what your ex really wants without speaking with his attorney," Jack advised. "Once I talk with him tomorrow we'll have a better picture. But I can assure you there's not a court in this land who'd give joint custody to a man who's been an absentee dad for all these years. Especially when the other parent is a fabulous mother."

Lexi found reassurance in Jack's words. And his support meant the world to her. But she wasn't convinced having him talk to Drew's attorney was the best move. Though she didn't have a lot of money in savings, she had some set aside for emergencies. It appeared now was the time to pull those dollars out of the bank and hire an attorney of her own.

"I appreciate the offer, Jack." Lexi spoke slowly, choosing her words carefully, not wanting to offend. "But I'm not sure you're the best one to make the call. You—"

"I *am* the best one, Lexi," Jack protested. "No one cares about you and Addie as much as I do."

"I understand that," Lexi said, holding up a hand. "But this is a high-powered law firm with some of the finest attorneys in Ohio—"

"I graduated from one of the top five law schools in the country. I'm considered one of the best family law attorneys in the United States." The words flowed from Jack's lips, bold and confident, as if he was arguing a case before a jury. "I can hold my own with any firm."

Lexi wasn't sure which of them was more surprised by the declaration.

"You're a lawyer?" she finally sputtered, breaking the shocked silence first.

"I am," he said hesitantly then more forcefully, with more sureness. "Yes, I am."

She met his gaze. "If you graduated from one of those schools, we should be able to look through pictures of past graduating classes and find you."

"I'm in no hurry." It might have been his imagination, but Jack sensed Lexi pulling back. She seemed afraid that once he discovered his true identity he'd be leaving her and Addie. Nothing could be further from the truth. Knowing his background would only enhance their life together in Jackson. He was sure of it.

So sure, in fact, that he wanted to talk about their future. But this wasn't the time. Not when she was still operating under the influence of migraine medicine. Besides, he needed more information for tomorrow's phone call. That had to be their priority tonight. "Tell me about Drew. How did you two first meet?"

"I don't want to talk about him," Lexi said. "I want to know what he wants and how to fight him."

"Humor me." Jack took her hand, relieved she didn't pull away. "Please."

After a long moment she sighed. "We were juniors in college. We met in a statistics class. He was acing the class and I...wasn't. He offered to tutor me. It wasn't long before we started dating."

"Was he a good boyfriend?"

Reluctantly Lexi nodded.

"You dated for what? Four years before you got pregnant? Did he change much during that time?"

"Not really." Lexi chewed on her lower lip. "Drew always knew what he wanted out of life. Once he finished his MBA, he was going to Oxford to get his doctorate. The plan was we'd marry and I'd go with him."

Jack's encouraging smile kept her talking.

"It was that last year of his MBA when things turned rocky." Lexi's lips tips upward. "I was finishing my master's in social work and loving it. I wanted to stay in the States and get a job. I didn't see why he had to go all the way to England for more school. Then I found out I was pregnant."

"That must have been hard."

"I was shocked. We'd always been so careful." Lexi paused for a second before continuing. "But we'd talked about getting married that summer anyway so although it was un-planned, I didn't think it was a big deal."

Jack could tell by the tone of her voice that Drew hadn't shared that opinion. "How did he react when you told him?"

"He blew up." Lexi exhaled a ragged breath. "He accused me of deliberately getting preg-nant in order to keep him in the U.S. He wanted me to have an abortion."

Jack bit back an expletive.

"I considered it," Lexi admitted in a barely audible voice. "But I couldn't." Her gaze dropped to her hands. "When I balked he told me if I had the baby, I was on my own."

"Bastard."

Lexi's chuckle held no humor. "True."

"You could have gotten child support," Jack

said. "He'd have had to pay whether he wanted to or not."

"I know," Lexi said with a sigh. "But I didn't want his money or the control it would give him over me. I managed on my own. I'm proud of that fact."

"You're a strong, amazing woman, Lexi Brennan." Jack brought her hand to his lips and kissed it.

"So how are we going to fight him?" she asked. "What's the strategy?"

"Tomorrow I call the law firm and see what he's really after," Jack said. "Until then we just sit tight."

"You won't let him take Addie from me?" The fear in her eyes tugged at his heartstrings.

"That's not even a possibility." Jack pulled

her to him and she rested her head against his chest. "Trust me. You don't have a thing to worry about."

## *Chapter Fourteen*

The next day at the hospital, Lexi worried more than she worked. She worried about Drew taking her daughter away. She worried what was going to happen when—not if—Jack found out his true identity. She worried how she and Addie would fare once he left.

In the four short weeks that he'd been in Jackson Hole, Jack had managed to carve a permanent place in her heart. What she felt for him made those long-ago feelings for Drew seem immature and childish. She hadn't loved Drew in a way that a woman should love a man she was about to marry. She certainly hadn't been the priority in his life. The fact that studying abroad had been more important to him than his fiancée and the life of his unborn child spoke volumes.

She glanced at the clock. Jack had set up a conference call with Drew and his attorney for two o'clock. It was one-fifty now and she had to be in a staff meeting from two to three. Then she had to head over to Addie's school for the annual spring music concert. Jack had already said he'd bum a ride into town and meet her there. Hopefully there would be a few minutes before the concert for them to talk.

Of course, she told herself, there was really nothing to discuss. The only way Drew was getting anywhere near her daughter was over her dead body.

\* \* \*

Jack hung up from his phone conversation with Milton Wessel, a partner in the law firm of Wessel and Sterns, feeling reassured. When Milt's secretary had called a little before two and asked if they could reschedule the call until three, Jack had been agreeable but suspicious that the delay was a power play. That was confirmed when he finally had the attorney on the phone and they tried to talk joint custody. Jack had simply laughed.

After that they'd gotten down to business. It quickly became clear that what Drew really wanted—and was prepared to fight for—was something the courts would give him anyway. Jack told the attorney he'd get back to him after speaking with his client. He hoped Lexi would be agreeable to the proposal but couldn't be certain of her response. When it came to Addie she was a tigress.

He glanced at the clock, then jammed the phone into his pocket and headed to the Wildwoods lobby to catch the shuttle. Addie's school was having a music concert this afternoon and he'd promised her he'd be there.

The van dropped Jack off in front of the school. He slipped through the double doors into the auditorium just as the first notes of the "Star Spangled Banner"—as interpreted by the first-year band students—filled the air. He quickly located Lexi, with an empty seat beside her, on the end of a row about halfway down.

Basking in the warmth of her welcoming smile, he slipped into the open seat next to her.

"I wasn't sure you were going to make it," Lexi whispered.

"Wouldn't have missed it for the world," he

whispered back, taking her hand. "I talked to the attorney."

Her eyes lit up. "What did he say?"

"Joint custody isn't even on the table." Jack wanted to tell her more but the curtains opened and the choral group—with Addie as the featured lower elementary vocal soloist—took the stage. For the next forty-five minutes, conversation was impossible.

After the concert concluded, the adults were herded into the school's common area for cookies and punch. Parents and students alike came up to compliment Addie on her performance.

Addie preened under all the compliments. But it warmed his heart when she insisted on holding his hand while drinking her punch.

"You're coming out to eat with us tonight, aren't you, Jack? I hope. I hope," Addie said when the principal announced that the students could leave with their parents.

"I wouldn't miss it, munchkin." Jack put the pads of his fingertips on top of her head and when she twirled, he laughed and wondered how any man could have given this up to study in England.

Dinner was pure torture for Lexi. Addie had a great time. Jack appeared relaxed. But all Lexi could think about was Jack's phone conversation with the attorney. It wasn't until they were back at her home and Addie was in bed that she and Jack could finally talk candidly.

She poured them each a glass of wine. Instead of sitting beside him on the sofa, she took a seat in the chair facing him. She leaned forward. "What did you find out? Tell me everything. Don't leave anything out."

Was it only her imagination or did Jack hesitate? "According to the attorney, Drew has felt badly about abdicating his parental responsibilities for some time."

"I bet," Lexi said with more than a little sarcasm.

"When he got your letter it stirred up those feelings," Jack continued in a matter-of-fact tone. "Apparently he married several years ago. When he voiced those regrets to his wife recently, she encouraged him to contact you."

"Does he have kids?" Lexi asked.

"No." Jack thought back to what the attorney had said. "They want children but have been unable to have any of their own."

"Well, I'm not giving him mine." The words came out so loud that even with the door closed, Jack was amazed Addie didn't wake up.

Still, he glanced in the direction of the bedrooms, waiting for the child to peer around the corner, and breathed a sigh of relief when she didn't. Lexi took another sip of wine and visibly fought for control of her emotions.

"He wants my daughter," she said in a more reasonable tone. "Is that pretty much the gist of it?"

"He doesn't want custody," Jack clarified. "And with his history of noninvolvement he wouldn't stand a chance anyway."

Lexi blew out a breath. "Thank God for that."

"But he is her father," Jack had to point out. "And, as her father, he does have certain rights."

"Rights?" Lexi snorted. "He gave up those when he told me to have an abortion. When he walked away from his daughter."

"Unfortunately the courts won't see it that way," Jack said in as gentle of a tone as he could muster. "They'll see a respected busi- nessman who made a mistake and now wants to make it right. They'll see a little girl who deserves to know her father."

"You're siding with them." Lexi's voice rose and her eyes flashed amber fire. "You think I should give him my child."

This time her anger was directed at *him.* But the pain in her eyes told Jack how hard the mere thought of visitation was for her. While he could sit back and view the situation im- partially, Lexi had lived through the tumul- tuous times of being abandoned and alone, not knowing if she'd be able to provide for her baby's needs.

"Come sit beside me," he said softly, patting the seat beside him.

For a second he thought she might do it, but

she crossed her arms and remained seated. "I'm fine right here."

He could feel a chasm growing wider between them. That scared him. For some reason she seemed to have gotten it in her head that he was siding with Drew. That couldn't be further from the truth. She and Addie's welfare were his priority.

Although this wasn't the most romantic time to confess his feelings, he had to make sure she knew how he felt. And the only way to do that was to say aloud the words he wasn't sure he had the right to say. "I love you, Lexi. I only want the best for you and Addie. This is *your* call. Not mine. I'll support—"

Before he could finish she was out of her chair and into his arms. "Oh, Jack, I love you, too."

For several heartbeats he just held her close,

feeling her soft curves pressed against him, smelling the sweet scent of her shampoo. A wave of emotion washed over him and he realized there was nothing he wouldn't do for her. Nothing he wouldn't give up. Drew might be a smart guy but he'd lost what truly mattered when he'd let this woman walk out of his life, when he'd turned his back on his own child.

"I'm scared, Jack," she whispered against his chest, so soft he barely heard the words. "I don't want him to come into her life only to hurt her."

Lexi was a reasonable woman. He had to make her see that this wasn't a fight she could win. But that wasn't the only reason she should agree. Addie needed to know her dad cared. Jack closed his eyes and said a little prayer. If he'd ever needed heavenly guidance, it was now. "Not knowing her father has already left a festering hole in Addie's heart. She told me her dad didn't like her. I could see it made her sad."

Lexi sighed but didn't lift her head from his chest. "I remember."

"I love Addie as if she was my very own, but she knows she has a dad out there. A father she's curious about, one she'd like to know."

"I'll kill him if he hurts her."

"Not if I get to him first," Jack said.

She chuckled. Or maybe it was a sob.

"We're only talking visitation," he said. "It could be supervised. You could be there with them, until you feel comfortable having them spend time alone."

Lexi lifted her head. "Drew would come all the way to Jackson Hole just to see her?"

"Yes," he said. "That's exactly how it would be."

"But then he'd want her to come to Ohio to see him."

"Probably. Eventually," Jack said, refusing to sugarcoat the facts. "But I made it very clear that if you agreed to let him come here, you're not committing to sending her there."

Tears filled her eyes. "I don't want her hurt."

"You and I, we'll make sure that doesn't happen."

A look of sadness swept across Lexi's face. "You'll be gone by the time Drew comes for a visit. Once you track down who you are, you'll go back to your law practice and to your family and friends."

Jack tightened his hold on her. "If you think you're getting rid of me that easily, you're mistaken. I don't need to know my name to know where I belong."

Lexi could hear the sincerity in his voice and knew he meant what he said. But once he knew his name, everything would change. She could only hope the change wouldn't bring disaster.

While waiting for Steve to arrive for their Friday night "work" session, Ellen strolled to her office window, a smile lifting the corners of her lips. Last night she and Steve had worked until after midnight on the Thompson case. It had been like old times. And beneath the professional discussion, there was a sizzle that both disturbed and excited her.

Steve liked her, not as a colleague or business associate but as a woman. She could see it in his eyes, feel it every time his hand *accidentally* brushed hers. But he'd never make a move until Nick was out of the picture. Steve wasn't the kind of guy to poach. In his mind she was still Nick's girlfriend. Ellen pressed her lips together. Nick, who'd left her high and dry for almost a month, without the courtesy of a single phone call to let her know he was okay.

As far as she was concerned, that constituted abandonment, which left her free to date whomever she wanted. And she wanted Steve.

She picked up the phone fully prepared to tell him just that when Anne, one of the paralegals, rushed into her office. "Ohmigod, Ellen, you'll never believe it. Nick is one of the featured stories on Yahoo."

Ellen stared, not sure she'd heard correctly.

"Open up Yahoo," the woman urged.

Ellen did as Anne suggested. She gasped. A big picture of Nick was under the headline Wyoming Skier Loses Memory in Avalanche.

"He doesn't know who he is," Anne said, her eyes sparkling behind her trendy black frames. "Crazy, huh? You've got to call and identify him. There's a contact name and phone number at the end of the article."

"Of course," Ellen murmured. She scanned the story and her heart flip-flopped in her chest. *No wonder he hasn't called me.*

Shame slid down her spine. Instead of being worried that something was wrong when she hadn't heard from Nick, she'd automatically assumed he was dissing her. What did that say about their relationship?

"What about Nick's father?" Anne asked. "Shouldn't someone notify Mr. Delacorte that his son has amnesia?"

Ellen glanced at her watch. "It's 6:00 a.m. in London. I'll ring him first and then call the sheriff."

"This is so exciting," Anne said with such verve that if she was a child Ellen knew she'd have clapped her hands.

"What's exciting?" Steve asked, strolling into her office. His eyes brightened the way they always did when he saw her. Ellen's heart flip-flopped in her chest the way it always did when she saw him.

"Nick was in an accident," Anne said. "He lost his memory but Ellen is going to Wyoming and bringing him home. Right, Ellen?"

Ellen's gaze locked with Steve's. Regret rose like bile in her throat. She nodded. "Right."

Since Addie was at a sleepover birthday party in Wilson, the minute she got home from work, Lexi and Jack began researching the top five law schools in the United States. It didn't take long to realize they would need to look at eight schools instead of five. Depending on the year, several schools moved in and out of the top five. Not knowing the year Jack had graduated added to the difficulty. But Lexi didn't mind. Though she knew it was selfish, the longer it took Jack to discover who he was, the longer she got to keep him with her.

After a couple of hours, she decided to take a break. "How did your session with Dr. Allman go?" Lexi pulled two tea bags out of the cupboard and set the kettle on the stove.

Jack looked up from the laptop. "Okay."

Dr. Allman was the psychologist who'd first evaluated Jack after his accident. He'd been pushing for him to return for a follow-up visit.

"Did he offer any explanation for why you can't remember your name?"

If she hadn't been looking at Jack, if she didn't know him so well, she might have missed the twist of his lips.

The teakettle began to whistle and she lifted

it from the burner but kept her gaze focused on him.

"Jack?" she pressed when he didn't respond.

"He thinks I don't want to remember."

Lexi pulled her brows together and absently poured the water into two cups. She'd always had a lot of respect for the psychologist but this comment seemed off-the-wall. "That doesn't make sense."

"It does to him." Jack sat back and wrapped his fingers around the cup she handed him. "He seems to think I'm scared of finding out who I am because then I'll have to make a choice."

"What kind of choice?" Lexi somehow managed to keep her voice steady despite the fact that her heart had lodged itself firmly in her throat.

"Staying or leaving." He rolled his eyes. "As if I'd leave you and Addie."

Lexi wasn't sure how to respond so she took a sip of tea, grateful when the phone rang and she could move to answer it.

"Hello?"

"Ms. Brennan?"

Lexi's fingers tightened around the receiver. The deep voice was familiar although she couldn't immediately place it.

"This is Sheriff Cassidy. Is John Doe, I mean Jack Snow, there?" the sheriff said in a conversational tone. "I tried the lodge but there was no answer in his room. Coraline told me I might find him at your place."

"Is something wrong?" Lexi choked out the words and out of the corner of her eye, she saw Jack push back his chair and rise, a question in his eyes.

"Absolutely not." The sheriff sounded almost jovial. "In fact, I'm calling with good news.

Our mystery man's fiancée saw his story on the Internet and called. John Doe's name is Nick Delacorte. He's an attorney out of Dallas. She's coming tomorrow to pick him up."

"Who is it?" Jack pressed.

"It's for you." She handed him the phone. "Your fiancée is on her way to Jackson to take you home."

Jack clicked the phone off and tried to smile. He didn't quite succeed. "Thank God they called before we wasted the whole evening doing all that research."

Lexi sank into the chair, not knowing how much longer her shaking legs could support her. "Tell me everything he said."

"My name is Nick Delacorte." Jack paced to the window and gazed outside. The name was somewhat familiar but still didn't seem to fit.

"I'm an attorney in Dallas. I supposedly have a fiancée, Ellen Kloss. She's flying on the corporate jet to Jackson tomorrow. That's all I know."

"Did he mention why they hadn't missed you before now?"

"Apparently I'd taken a monthlong vacation right before I came here. My father is working out of the London office. It sounds like he wasn't too concerned."

"And Ellen?" Lexi asked. "Was she concerned?"

If it was her and Jack hadn't contacted her in a day—much less a month—she'd be sick with worry.

"I guess." He shrugged. "I don't really know."

"You have a fiancée, Jack, I mean Nick." Lexi's voice began to rise despite her best efforts to control it. "How could you have forgotten about her?"

Nick raked his hand through his hair and turned to face her. "I don't know. But it doesn't matter."

"Of course it matters," Lexi snapped. "You told this woman you loved her. You asked her to marry you. That matters."

"I don't remember her." Nick took a step and closed his fingers around her shoulders. "If I once loved her, I don't anymore. I love you. It's *you* I want to be with."

Lexi longed to hold him tight and pretend they were the only two in the world. But she was a woman, not a child. She pulled away and wrapped her arms around herself. "That wouldn't be fair."

"To who?"

"To you. To her. To me." Lexi blinked back tears that threatened to spill and dropped her gaze to her hands. "I love you, Ja— Nick. But until you know who you are, you can't be a true partner to me."

"Lex, look at me," he demanded, his voice shaky. "I don't care what you call me, I love you. I don't want to lose what we have."

Lexi lifted her eyes. Before her stood the man she loved. She lifted a hand and touched his cheek. "I'm not going anywhere. Go to Dallas. Take the time to find out who you are and what you really want."

He grabbed her hand and pressed a kiss into her palm. "Come with me. You and Addie."

"I can't, Nick. This is something you have to do, something you have to decide on your own." She took in a deep breath and let it out slowly. "If you choose to stay with your fiancée, that's okay, too. All I want is for you to be happy."

He lifted his chin in a stubborn tilt. "I won't be happy if I'm not with you."

"Until you go back, until you find out who Nick Delacorte really is and what he wants, you won't be free to love me." Lexi somehow managed to keep her voice steady though inside her heart was breaking. "Not the way I deserve to be loved."

He stared at her for a long moment. "I'll do it. Not because I want to, only because you insist."

"Good." Somehow Lexi managed to keep the smile on her lips. When the letter from the law firm had followed so close on the heels of Mimi's abrupt change in wedding plans she'd found herself thinking the other shoe had dropped. But now she realized that what her grandmother used to say was true—bad news really did come in threes.

## Chapter Fifteen

If Nick thought begging would make a difference he'd be on his knees now. But the determined look on Lexi's face told him that he needed to comply with her wishes. "Just remember I'm leaving under protest," he said. "When I come back—and I will return—it will be with a diamond ring in my pocket."

The spark of joy in her eyes was so fleeting, he was left to wonder if it was only his imagination. Especially since her crossed arms and resolute expression gave nothing away.

"*Nick.* Please. Don't make any promises. Not to me. And especially not to Addie." Lexi's eyes sought his. "I know you believe in your heart that you'll be back. But that may change once you're in Dallas with your family and friends and…your fiancée."

Nick opened his mouth to protest but shut it without speaking. She was only trying to protect her child and her own heart. He couldn't fault her for either. But he also knew she had nothing to worry about. "I'll respect your wishes. I won't make any promises I can't keep. But I do need to speak with Addie before I leave."

"I can tell her goodbye for—"

"No." He held up a hand and shook his head.

"I refuse to leave town without explaining to her what's going on. I won't hurt her like that."

"Okay." Lexi collapsed into the chair like a balloon that had suddenly lost its air.

He wished he could pull her into his arms and console her, but he knew she wouldn't stand for it. "What time would be best for me to come by in the morning?"

"Whatever works for you," Lexi said. "I called Coraline earlier and took Saturday off."

His spirits brightened. "So you'll be available to take me to the courthouse?"

It was more a question than a statement. Lexi hated that he suddenly doubted her support.

"Of course I can." Though she wanted to spend every last second with him her heart clenched at the thought of witnessing the reunion scene between Nick and his fiancée. "But I won't go in with you."

The pain on her face told the story. Nick cursed Drew for hurting her and himself for doing the same thing. No, he told himself firmly, it wasn't the same. He wanted to stay. Drew had chosen to walk away.

"Can I spend the night?" If he had to leave tomorrow he wanted to stay as close as possible for as long as possible. "We don't have to make love. Just holding you would be enough."

"You have a fiancée. It wouldn't be right." Her expression was resolute but Nick saw the regret in her eyes.

"Can I at least have a hug?"

Lexi was about to refuse when the pleading look in his eyes changed her mind. This would be their goodbye and a last chance to feel his arms around her.

Apparently taking her silence for acquiescence, Nick took her fingers and drew her close. But when he leaned down to kiss her she turned her face, firmly reminding herself that he had a fiancée.

Still, when his lips brushed her cheek, Lexi closed her eyes, relishing the warm, intimate contact. This was the man she loved, the man she would love forever. Her heart broke at the realization that tomorrow he'd be gone. Maybe for good. She wrapped her arms around his shoulders one last time, resting her head against his neck.

After a heartbeat his arms joined around her waist and he pulled her tightly against him. "Wait for me. Promise you'll wait for me."

Lexi nodded. She told herself to step back but she remained where she was, unwilling to let him—and this moment—go. But in the end she would, because though he would deny it, they both knew he wasn't hers to keep.

Not yet.

* * *

Although Lexi was dressed, Addie was still in her pajamas when Nick arrived at the cabin early the next morning. Though the morning air held a decided chill, thanks to the fire in the hearth the inside of the cabin was toasty warm.

"Let me take your coat." Lexi moved to his side as he pushed the door shut behind him.

The color of her sweater made her eyes look like warm honey and when she leaned close for his coat, she smelled like cinnamon. Though a welcoming smile sat on her lips, her eyes held no joy.

Knowing he was the cause of her sadness pierced like a knife to his heart.

"Jack," Addie called out from the sofa, where she was sitting with a book. Her face brightened when she saw him. "Mommy is making blueberry pancakes this morning. They're my favorite."

"Mine, too," he said.

"Since when?" Lexi asked.

"Since right now," he said, feeling relieved when she smiled.

"Can I help?" She'd returned to the stove and he slipped to stand behind her, peering over her shoulder as she poured the batter onto the griddle.

"I've got it under control." She lowered her voice. "I told Addie about her dad."

"How did she take it?" he asked in a barely audible tone.

"I'm not sure." Lexi's brows drew together. "I hoped maybe you—"

"Let me know if you change your mind and need anything," he called out loudly over his shoulder as he headed to the sofa. "I'm going to keep Addie company."

Nick paused at the edge of the sofa. Though the book was open on the child's lap, he swore she hadn't turned a page since he'd arrived. "What are you reading?"

"Junie B. Jones," Addie said without much enthusiasm.

"Mind if I sit?" He glanced pointedly at a spot on the sofa next to her. "If there's enough room?"

"There's lots," Addie said, scootching to the middle so he could sit next to her.

"Your mother told me the exciting news."

Addie cocked her head.

"I understand your father wants to come to Jackson and meet you."

Addie lowered her gaze to the book on her lap.

"What do you think about that?"

Addie lifted a shoulder in a slight shrug.

"Did your mom tell you I have some exciting news of my own?"

"What is it?"

"I found out my real name," he said, trying to summon up some enthusiasm. "I'm Nick, not Jack. And I'm going to meet my father, too."

"You don't know your daddy?"

"I don't remember him." Nick kept his tone light. "It will be like meeting him for the first time, kind of like you and your father."

Addie pondered his words for several heart-beats. "What if he doesn't like you?"

"I've thought about that," Nick admitted. He wasn't lying. Last night when he was in bed trying to sleep he'd wondered how today would go. "I guess if he doesn't, that will be sad but okay. I have other people in my life who like me."

"Me an' Mommy like you," Addie said.

"That means a lot to me."

"And if my daddy doesn't like me—"

"Then you still have your mother and me and Coraline and Sarah and Mary Karen and—"

"You're silly." Addie giggled and the clouds lifted from her eyes.

"You're lucky," Nick said. "Your daddy is coming all the way to Wyoming to see you. I have to go to Dallas to see mine."

"Breakfast is ready," Lexi announced.

"When?" Addie demanded. "When are you going to meet your daddy?"

Nick slowly stood, the sudden heaviness in his heart weighing him down. "Today."

"Wait." Addie jumped to her feet and headed for the hall. "I'll be right back."

"Addie," Lexi protested. "The pancakes will get cold."

"Just a minute, Mommy," Addie answered without breaking stride.

Nick was just pulling out a chair when she returned. Dangling from her fingers was a gold heart-shaped locket. She pressed it into his hand. "This is for you."

Lexi's mouth formed a perfect O.

"What is it?" he asked as Addie scrambled up on the new bar stool that he'd bought with the last of his cash. At the time it had made sense. After all, if they were going to eat together as a family, they needed three chairs, not two. And doggone it, it still made sense.

"Open it," Addie urged.

With suddenly clumsy fingers, Nick found the latch on the side and the locket swung open.

Inside were two tiny pictures. One of Addie. One of Lexi. "This is beautiful."

"It's Mommy and me," Addie said. "You wouldn't want to put it around your neck like I do because you're a boy. But you can put it in your pocket. When you meet your daddy today, we'll be there with you."

It took several attempts before Nick could swallow past the large lump in his throat. He probably shouldn't take it—after all, the necklace was obviously special to her—but as he slipped it into his pocket he realized suddenly how better prepared he felt to face a group of strangers. "Thank you, Addie. I'll take good care of it."

His gaze met Lexi's and she smiled approvingly.

Once they were all settled around the breakfast bar they said grace and then dug into the pancakes.

"How long will you be gone?" Addie asked around a mouthful of pancakes.

Nick could feel Lexi's eyes on him. "I'm not sure."

"But you'll call us, right?" Addie asked. "When Mommy had to go out of town for a meeting, she called me every night so I wouldn't worry."

Lexi set her fork on the plate. "Honey, Nick might not have time—"

"I'll call." Nick ignored Lexi's censuring look. He'd told her he wouldn't make promises he couldn't keep. But this was one promise he was looking forward to keeping.

Addie had wanted to ride with them into town. That was, until Coraline called with the news that Sarah and her parents were at the lodge. The seven-year-old suddenly decided that hanging out with her friend was more fun than a car ride into town. Although she did give Nick a big hug when they dropped her off at the lodge.

"I'm glad Addie didn't come." Lexi pulled off Simpson Street into the parking lot of the Teton County Courthouse where the Sheriff's office was located. A couple of tears slipped down her cheeks but she hurriedly wiped them aside before Nick could notice. "I think it would be hard for her to say goodbye."

"I know it's hard for me," Nick said in a husky voice. She'd barely turned off the ignition when he reached over and took her hand. "I don't want to leave Addie. Or you."

Her heart turned to mush. For a second Lexi feared she would lose control. But she swallowed a couple of times, blinked rapidly for several seconds until the urge to break down and sob subsided.

"I don't want you to leave, either," she said finally when she found her voice. "But it's the right thing to do. Just like having Addie meet her father."

His thumb caressed her palm. "Even while I'm gone I want to stay involved in those negotiations."

"Are you sure?" Lexi sputtered, finding it difficult to concentrate with his nearness assaulting her senses.

"Just because I'm leaving town for a little while doesn't mean I no longer care." He glanced at the courthouse then down at his watch. "I'd better go inside."

"Good luck with—"

Suddenly his lips were on hers. The hard, fierce kiss left her head spinning.

"I'll be back," he said. "You can count on that."

The phone rang just before Addie's eight o'clock bedtime.

"It's Jack." The child scrambled up from her seat in front of the television to grab Lexi's cell. "I mean, Nick."

Lexi prayed it *was* him calling. Not only because she wanted to hear his voice but because her daughter's heart would be broken if he didn't call as promised.

"Hello." Addie's face lit up like a hundred-watt bulb. "How was your daddy?"

Lexi let out the breath she'd been holding. Nick had called.

He'd kept his promise.

She leaned back against the sofa, her knees weak with relief.

"Put him on speaker, Addie." Lexi couldn't keep the smile from her lips. "I want to hear all about his day, too."

"How are my girls?" Nick's rich baritone filled the room.

"We're fine," Addie answered. "'Cept Mommy cut her finger. She cried and cried."

"Are you okay, Lex?" Even across the airwaves, his concern came across loud and clear.

"It was nothing. I was slicing some French bread and nicked my finger." It had hurt a little. But once she'd started crying it had been hard to stop. And though she wasn't about to admit it aloud, she knew most of the tears had little to do with the cut finger. "No big deal."

"What about your dad?" Addie pressed, returning to her original question.

"I had your locket in my pocket when I went to meet him," Nick said. "I kept thinking about you two as I walked up the steps to his home."

"What is he like?" Lexi asked.

"He seems nice. It was strange to meet someone who's my dad and not know him at all."

"Did you like him?" Addie probed.

"I think so," Nick said. "But it's like what you and I talked about that day in the gym. Sometimes it takes time to get to know someone and like them. It doesn't always happen right away."

They talked for a while longer before Lexi sent Addie off to bed and switched the phone off speaker. "How is Ellen?"

"Well, for starters she's not my fiancée."

"Oh, Nick, please tell me you didn't break off the engagement already. You didn't even give her a—"

"We were never engaged," he said quickly. "She told the sheriff that because she thought it would give her more credibility when she called."

Lexi collapsed against the back of the sofa. "Were you even dating?"

"We were," he said. "Apparently we'd been dating for six months. Both of us agreed it was time for things between us to either move to the next level or call it quits. I remember coming to Jackson Hole to ski and make some decisions about our future."

"It seems odd you wouldn't be making that decision together."

"Yeah, I know."

"Where were you staying before your accident?" Lexi propped her feet up on the coffee table. For a second it was easy to believe he was simply away on a business trip and calling home to check in. "The sheriff couldn't find you registered at any of the motels in the area."

"I was using a friend's condo in Teton Village," Nick said. "Tony picked me up at the airport, gave me the keys to his place then after dropping me off, he headed to Europe."

"What about the money?" Lexi asked, trying to think of all the questions that had puzzled them both. "Why did you have so much on you?"

"I've always liked to carry cash," he said. "I never was one for credit cards."

"What about the stone building with the bell tower?" she asked. "Was that an old high school or college?"

He laughed. "It's the church we attend. And the wedding I remembered was of some mutual friends. Ellen was a bridesmaid. I was the best man."

"Sounds like you're starting to remember more," Lexi said, her heart clenching at the realization of how closely his and Ellen's lives were intertwined. They might not be engaged but they were on the verge of formalizing their relationship before he left Texas. "Returning to Dallas has been a good thing."

"I miss you, Lexi," he said. "I can't begin to tell you how much."

*Me, too,* she wanted to say, but pressed her lips together instead.

"Tell me what's on the agenda for tomorrow," she said.

"Church and brunch with my father and Ellen. I'm not sure what else," he said. "I'll call you tomorrow night and tell you how it went."

"You don't have to—"

"I want to." His voice lowered to a husky whisper. "I love you, sweetheart."

"Nick, don't." But she was so greedy to hear the words that her protest sounded weak even to her own ears.

"Don't what? Love you? That's not possible."

"Good night, Nick." She knew he was waiting to hear the words from her lips but kept her mouth shut. Words could be chains. She wanted him to be free to find what made him happy without feeling tied to her and the promises he'd made.

But when his end went silent and she was certain he'd hung up, with the phone cradled in her palm, she poured out all the words she couldn't say minutes ago.

Nick sat on the bed in his luxury condo in downtown Dallas and flipped open Addie's locket. He smiled. When he and Lexi had first spoken tonight, she'd seemed a bit distant. But right when their conversation appeared to be over, she'd finally started talking—about how much he meant to her and how hard it had been for her to let him leave. He'd opened his mouth to respond when it suddenly struck him that she didn't know he was still there. She was saying all those words she couldn't say because she was afraid it would influence the way he felt about Ellen, about Dallas, about his old life.

Silly woman. She didn't realize that she and Addie were his life now. The only place he wanted to be was with them. Still, because it was important to her, he'd stay in Texas until he got all his memory back. Then he'd be hopping the corporate jet back to Jackson Hole and the woman he loved.

They'd figure out the rest…together.

## Chapter Sixteen

"Is it coming back to you?" Ellen asked when they'd returned to his office that Monday after a tour of the entire floor.

Nick just smiled.

"And what about me? Am I a little more familiar?"

Nick let his gaze linger. With honey-colored hair to her shoulders, big blue eyes and long shapely legs, Ellen was an attractive woman. He could see why a man would be attracted to her. But when she stood close—like she was now—there wasn't even the slightest spark of electricity between them. Very puzzling, especially considering they'd been dating for six months. "It's coming," he said with a grin when he realized she expected an answer. "At a snail's pace, but it's coming."

He glanced at his mahogany desk. "I remember sitting in this office, making calls, working on cases and looking out the windows over the Dallas skyline."

"Well, I guess that's something," she said with a rueful smile.

"Let's go to lunch."

Her perfectly arched blonde brows drew together. "It's only eleven."

"We'll beat the crowd," he said. "You pick the place."

"Hanabi is good." Penny, his secretary,

waltzed into the room and dropped a stack of files on his desk.

"Hanabi?"

"It's sushi," Ellen said. "You don't like sushi."

Like a comet a memory flashed, shining brightly for a second then fading just as quickly. "But *you* like it. Right?"

Ellen hesitated. "Well, I—"

"She's eaten there every week since you've been gone," Penny said then shut her mouth at Ellen's warning glance.

"Let's give it a try," Nick said.

"Before you both leave," Penny said. "I want to remind you that Mrs. Rediger's retirement party is today from eleven to one in the large conference room."

Nick waited until Penny had left the office before turning to Ellen. "Mrs. Rediger?"

"She's been your father's secretary for thirty years," Ellen explained. "His right arm."

"Will my dad be there?" Nick had spent most of Sunday with his father catching up. Awkward at first, by the evening they were fairly comfortable with each other. Only now did Nick realize they hadn't discussed if his father would be in the office today.

"Mrs. Rediger told me he's in Austin today." Ellen lowered her voice to a whisper. "I think she was disappointed he was going to miss her reception, especially since he's back from London."

"Well, then, we'd better stop at the reception before we leave for lunch," Nick said.

"Are you serious?"

Nick took her arm. "I wouldn't miss it for the world."

Nick had shut off all the lights in his condo and now sat in the darkened living room with the shades open and the lights of the city spread out before him. He'd just finished telling Lexi about his day.

"I bet his secretary was thrilled you came to her party," Lexi said.

"She seemed happy." Nick couldn't understand why Mrs. Rediger kept thanking him, when she was the one who'd given thirty years of service to the firm. She'd started to cry when he'd told her as much.

"What did you do after that?" Lexi asked.

"Ellen and I went to lunch at this sushi place not far from the office."

"It surprises me that you like sushi."

"That's what Ellen said, but I remembered she did, so I thought I'd give it a try."

"That was…nice," Lexi said, a catch in her voice. "How'd you like it?"

"Ugh," he said, smiling when Lexi laughed.

"If I ask you a question, will you tell me the truth?"

"You can ask me anything. I'll always tell you the truth."

"Do you think I'm a nice person?"

"Of course you are. Why do you even ask?"

"Well, Ellen seemed surprised that I'd go to the sushi place with her."

"And?"

"Mrs. Rediger and the rest of the staff made such a big deal that I'd come to her party. It was as if they didn't expect to see me there." Nick paused and reminded himself that this was Lexi. There was nothing he couldn't say to her. "I'm getting the feeling I wasn't a very nice guy."

"I don't for one minute believe that," Lexi said, her indignation making him smile. "You have a good heart, Nick. That's not something that changes."

Her words buoyed his sagging spirits. He took a sip of wine. "Enough about me. Tell me what's going on in your life."

"You'll never guess who's back in town."

"Who?"

"Mimi and her new husband. I ran into them at the supermarket."

"How's she doing?" Nick took another sip of wine and relaxed against the back of his chair. He'd looked forward to this call all day. Even talking about day-to-day things with Lexi was special.

"Mimi seems happy," Lexi said. "And her new husband appears to be a genuinely nice guy. I don't think she regrets wasting money on those flowers and invitations one bit."

"Speaking of invitations," he said. "My secretary, Penny, is getting married. I told her about the Web site we'd found and she checked it out. It sure brought back the memories."

"I had a lot of fun picking out those invitations," Lexi said with a sigh then yipped. "I didn't realize it was this late. I'd better get to bed. Take care, Nick."

"I love you, Lexi," he said, but she'd already clicked off and the words fell into dead air.

Nick continued to call Lexi and Addie every night for the next two weeks. Each day more and more of his memory was returning. By the end of the second week all of it had come back with the exception of his relationship with Ellen.

He remembered spending time with her but the emotional aspects of their relationship still eluded him. Lexi had told him to stay in Dallas until he knew who he was, but he was impatient to return to Jackson Hole. Addie was set to meet her father for the first time next week and he wanted to be there to support both her and her mother.

Lexi had been quieter than usual on the phone and he sensed her insecurities were playing with her head. He worried that it wouldn't be long before she'd start pushing him away to protect herself.

Nick wasn't about to let that happen. He glanced at his watch. Five o'clock. It was time to pay Ellen a visit. He couldn't believe he hadn't thought of this earlier. While the thought of kissing a woman other than Lexi felt wrong in so many ways, he had to give it a try. He needed to go home to Lexi a free man. There was only one way to do it.

Ellen's outer office was deserted so Nick

opened her door and stuck his head inside. She stood alone, gazing out the window. Since he'd returned she'd been at his side constantly, helping and encouraging him. But he sensed her heart wasn't in it. Or maybe it was that *his* heart wasn't in it. "May I come in?"

She turned and smiled at the sound of his voice. "As if you need to ask."

He moved to her side, then took his time, determined not to rush. Reaching up, Nick gently touched her face, pulling her chin and her mouth up to his. He brushed his lips against hers in a chaste kiss. When she didn't pull away, he kissed her again, still gently but with a question, waiting for her to respond, waiting for his body to react.

"Get away from her."

Strong hands jerked him back. Strong hands

that belonged to Steve Laughlin, one of the attorneys in the firm.

"If you think you can walk away from her like she doesn't matter then come back and pick up where you left off, you're wrong. Ellen is too good for you."

Out of the corner of his eye, Nick saw Ellen's eyes begin to shine. He smiled.

"You think this is funny?" Steve's voice rose. "You—"

"I think my experiment worked," Nick said.

"What experiment?" Steve and Ellen said in the same breath.

"I like Ellen and I admire her," Nick said. "That's all. When I kissed her I realized I'd never felt anything more for her than friendship. That's why I couldn't remember loving her because those feelings were never there."

"They were never there for me, either. I cared

about you. I liked you. But I didn't love you," Ellen said. "So it looks like you can go back to your dark-haired woman in Jackson Hole with a clear conscience."

At his look of surprise she smiled. "I saw the way you kissed her in the car before you came into the courthouse."

"I love her," he said. "Just like you love Steve."

Ellen's cheeks pinked but she didn't deny it.

Jack smiled. The past had been addressed and put to bed. Now he could finally do what he'd wanted to do for the past two weeks…head back to Jackson Hole and Lexi.

## Chapter Seventeen

"What do you mean you don't need me to work today?" Lexi stood at the door to the Wildwoods kitchen dumbfounded to see that Coraline already had the breakfast preparation well in hand. "This is my Saturday to work. And I'm completely free. Mary Karen called last night and picked up Addie this morning for a nature walk around Jenny Lake."

Coraline's lips curved upward as if she found Lexi's protests amusing. "Go home and clean your house, then. Or give yourself a manicure. I'm sure you can find something to keep you busy."

Lexi raised a hand to her head. While most people would kill for a day off, she needed to keep busy. Last night she'd talked to Nick. That in itself wasn't unusual, since he'd called every night since he'd left Jackson Hole. But he'd been happy, almost euphoric. Before he'd gotten off the phone he'd let it slip that he was going out with Ellen and a bunch of friends from the office.

That's when Lexi knew he'd made his decision. It wouldn't be long before he quit calling and embraced his new life fully.

*No,* her heart argued, *he loves me.*

"Lexi."

She looked up to find Coraline standing beside her, a concerned look in her eyes. "Are you okay?"

"I— It's just been hard since Nick left," Lexi admitted. "It helps if I keep busy. So is it okay if I hang around and help you this morning?"

"Honey, any other time would be fine," Coraline said. "But today I feel like being alone in the kitchen. You understand."

Lexi nodded, though she didn't understand at all. "I guess I'll check and see if they need help in the dining room."

"We're fully staffed today." Coraline took her arm and turned her toward the door. "Go home, Lexi. Really, just go home."

Several pity tears slid down Lexi's cheeks but Coraline didn't appear to notice, or if she did, she didn't comment. Lexi trudged back to the cabin with a heavy heart. When she got there she noticed an envelope wedged in the door.

Her name was on the front written with a calligraphy pen. Lexi didn't have to open the envelope to know what it was and who it was from. When she'd run into Mimi a couple days earlier, the new bride hinted she'd be interested in a post-wedding bridal shower. Lexi hadn't offered to host but it appeared Mimi had found some other sucke— er, friend, to have one for her.

Lexi reached into her pocket for her house key but when she went to put it in the lock, the door swung open. She hesitated only a second. She'd been running late when she'd left and must have forgotten to close it fully.

She'd barely pushed the door open when her heart slammed against her ribs. Standing in her living room, dressed in a hand-tailored suit, Ferragamo tie and Italian loafers that probably cost more than she made in a month stood the love of her life. "Nick."

"I wondered when you'd get back." He smiled, caressing her with his eyes.

She wished she'd taken more time with her appearance this morning. Next to his splendor she felt underdressed in her khakis, white button-down shirt and short yellow cardigan. "I was supposed to work but—"

"Coraline sent you home."

"How did you know—" Lexi paused. "She knew you were here, didn't she?"

He smiled and took a step closer.

Lexi shivered. Her gaze settled hungrily over him. "Addie's going to be sorry she missed you. She's on a nature walk with Mary Karen."

"I know." He moved closer, so near she could see the familiar flecks of gold in his eyes and smell the intoxicating spicy scent of his cologne. "What do you have in your hand?"

She blinked, feeling unsteady. "An invitation."

He took another step closer. "Aren't you going to open it?"

"Sure, yeah, I guess." Lexi fumbled with the envelope, her trembling fingers making the simple task impossible. In frustration she finally gave up. "I'll open it later."

She didn't want to fool with Mimi's invitation when she had much more important things occupying her thoughts. Like Nick and why he was here. In her house. Today.

"Let me help you." He quickly slipped it open and pulled the card from the envelope, his eyes never leaving her face. "What does it say?"

Her gaze settled on a large bouquet of long-stemmed white roses in a crystal vase on her breakfast bar. "Are those for me?"

He didn't even glance in that direction. "Read the card."

Lexi glanced briefly at the lettering then back up at Nick. "Mimi got something right. This is my favorite font."

"What does it say?" he prompted. "Come on, Lex. Read it aloud."

Why was he so insistent?

She cast another glance at the flowers then focused on the card.

*"Nicholas Edward Delacorte pledges his love for all eternity and respectfully requests the honor of Lexi Anne Brennan's hand in marriage.*

*Mr. Delacorte further requests the privilege of becoming Addison Marie Brennan's stepfather."*

Lexi lifted tear-filled eyes to Nick. "*You* remembered the font. And the flowers."

Nick's smile dropped. "Is that all you have to say?"

"What about Ellen? And Dallas?"

"Ellen and I were never in love. We both recognize that now. She has a great guy in the office who *does* love her. I wouldn't be surprised to hear wedding bells in the future." Nick smiled with satisfaction. "Dallas, well, it's good. But I like it here, too. I thought we could live here and I could work remote, flying back to Dallas whenever necessary. If I end up being gone too much—"

"We can work that out later." Lexi waved a dismissive hand, her invitation to be Nick's wife clutched in her tight grip. "It doesn't matter where we live as long as we're together."

Reaching into his pocket, Nick pulled out a tiny black box and flicked it open. The large emerald-cut diamond caught and scattered the overhead light.

He took her hand and gazed into her eyes. "Lexi, I love you with all my heart. I love Addie as if she was my own daughter. I promise if you give me the opportunity, I'll be a great husband and father...because that's what you both deserve."

Lexi blinked.

He took that as a sign that he should continue. "When I left here, you told me after I found myself I could come back to you. I now know who I am. And what I want hasn't changed since the day I met you."

"Oh, Nick, are you sure?"

"I thank God for all the events in my life that brought me to this point. I wouldn't be the man I am now if I hadn't met you. I would be both happy and honored if you would accept my proposal."

Tears streamed down her cheeks. "I don't know what to say."

For the first time he felt a stab of fear. He couldn't lose Lexi now that he'd found her. "'Yes' would be good."

An impish gleam filled her eyes. "I'm a traditional kind of gal but I like nontraditional, too. After all, I fell in love with a man before I knew his name."

Nick's eyes remained focused on her face. "What are you saying?"

"That I'd like to accept your offer of marriage while we're in bed…with you wearing nothing but this tie and me wearing nothing but this beautiful diamond."

She held out her hand.

He dutifully slid the ring onto her left finger.

Then suddenly Nick was laughing with relief and kissing her over and over again. "Say yes."

"You have to get naked first," she said with an impudent smile and sprinted down the hall, clothes dropping with each step.

By the time they hit the bed there was only a tie, a ring and a whole lot of love between them.

# *Epilogue*

*2 months later*

Addie pointed to the top of the wedding cake that held three figures instead of two. "That's me and Mommy and Nick. He's my new daddy. We're a family now."

"Cool." Connor Vaughn eyed the cake. "When can we eat it?"

"First you have to cut it with that pretty knife."

"Okay." Connor grinned. "I can do that."

* * *

"Ohmigod, Lexi." Mary Karen rushed to where Lexi stood underneath a bower of spring flowers, sipping champagne with her new husband and visiting with David and July Wahl. "I'm so sorry. I swear he was out of my sight for only one second."

"Let me guess," David said with a chuckle. "Connor strikes again."

Travis followed behind with a defiant but obviously scared Connor. "You, my man," he said to the boy, "are in deep do-do."

Lexi smiled, not at all concerned. "What happened?"

"Connor cut your wedding cake." Two bright spots of pink dotted Mary Karen's cheeks. "He and Addie were feeding it to each other."

"I hope the photographer got some good pictures," Nick said, taking a sip of champagne.

"I didn't mean to do anything wrong." Addie's brow was furrowed in worry and her chin quivered. "We cut it just like you and Nick did at the wedding last week."

Lexi understood her daughter's confusion. In a traditional vein, last week she and Nick had been married at his family church in Dallas—the large stone one with the bell tower. She'd worn a beautiful ivory-colored wedding dress. Addie had been a flower girl. The wedding of her dreams had been pulled together in record time with the help of Ellen, Penny and Mrs. Rediger who, as mother to six girls, had an amazing abundance of contacts in the wedding industry.

The fact that Nick wanted to introduce her to his family and friends and give her the wedding she thought she'd never have had meant the world to her. But she'd come to realize it wasn't the ceremony but the man at her side, as well as sharing their special day with family and friends, that made the ceremony special. That was why they'd decided to do it all over again, only this time in Jackson Hole.

"I'm so sorry," Addie wailed.

"It's okay, sweetie." Nick leaned down and picked up Addie. "Cake is made to be eaten. How is it?"

"Yummy," Addie said, the gold heart-shaped locket gleaming in the summer sun.

Connor nodded his agreement.

Lexi smiled. "Rachel is going to cut the cake for us. Why don't you both go see if you can help hand it out?"

"You might regret that," Mary Karen said.

"It's only cake," Lexi said. "This day is about love and being happy." She paused for a moment, catching sight of Drew and his wife talking with Nick's dad.

She was glad they'd invited Drew. Today wasn't about the past but about the future, a future that had never looked brighter.

"You're looking awfully serious, Mrs. Delacorte." Nick touched the side of her face, his eyes as gentle as his fingers.

"I was thinking." She slipped her hand into his and it felt like coming home. This was what marriage was all about—one man, one woman and a love strong enough to last a lifetime.

"Let me guess. You were thinking how good I'll look later wearing nothing but this." He glanced down at his shirtfront.

Lexi laughed and grabbed his tie, pulling him to her for a kiss. "That, too."

\* \* \* \* \*

*Discover Pure Reading Pleasure with*

## Visit the Mills & Boon website for all the latest in romance

**Buy** all the latest releases, backlist and eBooks

**Find out** more about our authors and their books

**Join** our community and chat to authors and other readers

**Free** online reads from your favourite authors

**Win** with our fantastic online competitions

**Sign** up for our free monthly eNewsletter

**Tell us** what you think by signing up to our reader panel

**Rate** and review books with our star system

# www.millsandboon.co.uk

 Follow us at twitter.com/millsandboonuk

 Become a fan at facebook.com/romancehq

Mas

| 1 | 2 | 3 | | 5 | 6 | 7 | 8 | 9 | 10 |
|---|---|---|---|---|---|---|---|---|---|
| 11 | 12 | 13 | 14 | 15 | 16 | 17 | 18 | 19 | 20 |
| 21 | 22 | 23 | 24 | 25 | 26 | 27 | 28 | 29 | 30 |
| 31 | 32 | 33 | 34 | 35 | 36 | 37 | 38 | 39 | 40 |
| | 42 | 43 | 44 | 45 | 46 | 47 | 48 | 49 | 50 |
| | 52 | 53 | 54 | 55 | 56 | 57 | 58 | 59 | 60 |
| | 62 | 63 | 64 | 65 | 66 | 67 | 68 | 69 | 70 |
| | | 73 | 74 | 75 | 76 | 77 | 78 | 79 | 80 |
| | | 83 | 84 | 85 | 86 | 87 | 88 | 89 | 90 |
| | | 93 | 94 | 95 | 96 | 97 | 98 | 99 | 100 |
| | | 103 | 104 | 105 | 106 | 107 | 108 | 109 | 110 |
| | | 113 | 114 | 115 | 116 | 117 | 118 | 119 | 120 |
| | | | | | 126 | 127 | 128 | 129 | 130 |
| | | | | | 136 | 137 | | 139 | 140 |
| | | | | | | | | 149 | 150 |
| | | | | | | | | 159 | |